TAMING HIS BRAT

Daddy Takes the Reins Book 2

KESSILY LEWEL

✿ Created with Vellum

CHAPTER 1

Settling into his home had been easier than she'd expected. Maybe the sweet memories she had from their previous attempt at a relationship had helped to ease the way this time. It certainly wasn't because of some mythical honeymoon period where every problem was easily solved, and they didn't get on each other's nerves.

No, with Sam there were always going to be sparks and moving in together didn't erase the fact that they tended to rile each other up. She wasn't even sure she'd want to lose that. Some of their hottest nights had come after long days of snapping at each other until they both had enough.

But still, moving into his small cabin and getting used to living with someone intimately was new for her. She'd thought there would be more issues. So far things seemed to be going surprisingly well. Well, *she* was surprised anyway. Sam had been telling her all along things would be fine and she was overthinking.

That was her gift, overthinking a problem until it ended up ten times worse, but for the first time in her life she had real incentive to avoid that path. Things were good with Sam and she didn't want to mess them up this time.

Never once had she thought they'd end up back together. And they probably wouldn't have, if her dad's will hadn't forced the issue. They'd fought a lot. But now... now things were working.

His strong need to protect and nurture had always been there, they'd just never had a name for it. But once she'd gotten used to calling him Daddy, at least when she was in trouble, she'd been amazed at how comfortable it felt. It filled a need for both of them and she'd grown to love the way it felt to snuggle in his arms and whisper *Daddy* in his ear.

Sam was reasonable and was willing to let her have a say in things. That helped. The change in their relationship helped more. She'd willingly given him control over her and he'd stepped into a new role as her Daddy. She honestly found that easier than letting him run the ranch, but with him bossing her somehow it helped to deal with that too—a little.

There was still conflict. She'd spent years planning what she'd do once the ranch was hers and seeing him making all the big decisions grated sometimes. He was only a couple of years older than she was, but he'd been the ranch foreman for years when her father was alive, and he knew what he was doing.

Once her emotions had calmed down and she left them out of the equation, she had to admit he knew a lot more than she did about how things were run. But he was old school, like her father. He kept to the way things had always been done, whereas she thought the ranch could do with a few modernizations and they'd clashed over it a few times before she'd finally backed down.

She was no longer sure which of them was more stubborn. But she did know that committing to a relationship with him meant she had better watch her tone when she made suggestions. When she kept her temper under control, did her research, and discussed it with him reasonably, she was more likely to get him to bend.

When she didn't, she was likely to be the one bending. As in bending over the nearest piece of furniture so he could paddle her ass. Working with a Dom wasn't easy, at least not for her. She had trouble with her mouth when she got upset and Sam had taken to the role of Daddy like he'd been born to it.

She got away with exactly as much as he felt like letting her, and then he tugged those reins tight and pulled her back into place. Sometimes she wondered if he considered her some unbroken filly that he needed to train to the saddle. A lot of times she wondered that actually, especially when he got out the crop and placed a few dozen red welts across her ass because she didn't obey him.

And she loved it. It was what she'd asked for. He'd been the one to hold back in the beginning. At first convinced she shouldn't be making important decisions while grieving. Later he had his own conditions, but they'd worked it out finally.

She'd gotten everything she needed, most of what she wanted, and it was all going perfectly. It worried her a little because in her experience things didn't go well for long before something messed them up. But until that happened, she was just going to try to enjoy what she had.

She looked up at the clock and winced. It was nearly quitting time on the ranch. The hands would be heading home, and Sam would lock the gate behind them. Then he'd come to check on her and enjoying what she had might become a problem. Because what she had was a strict Daddy, with a hard hand, who had told her that he wanted the last of her stuff unpacked before he got home.

He probably thought she was delaying because she still had doubts, but the truth was a lot simpler. She hated unpacking and organizing things. He'd made as much space as he could for her stuff, but the place was small and there just wasn't going to be enough room. So, part of unpacking was deciding what she needed and what could be stored for a while.

It was a lot of work, and some of it was emotional so she'd put it off. But she'd been living in his house for almost two months now, while they tripped over boxes and bags every time they moved. Sam liked things neat and uncluttered so that didn't work for him and her ass was on the line if she couldn't get it done.

He'd reminded her, then he'd warned her. Finally, he'd put his foot down and given her a deadline of a week to sort things out. She'd worked on it a little, but it was easy to get distracted and drop something she didn't want to be doing. Now it was coming down to the wire and she was out of time.

There was always that urge to test him. She liked bringing out the Daddy side of him by disobeying, but she had a feeling he was already at his limit with this one. Besides she was getting a little tired of bruising her shins every time she bumped into something.

There was a specific muscle in his jaw that jumped visibly every time he came home and tripped over something. That meant there was a good chance it wouldn't be just a short spanking, or one she could nudge over to sexy times. The part of her that wanted to see what would happen, was quickly stomped down by the part that enjoyed sitting comfortably.

She came to the decision that she definitely didn't want to be in trouble when Sam walked in the door. Which made it all the more unfortunate that she'd put things off for too long, and she simply ran out of time to finish. She'd planned to make a real effort that day, but something had come up and distracted her. She'd gotten back to it much later, but she was still working on the final box when she heard him cleaning off his boots on the porch.

The thudding of work boots as he used the bristled scraper outside was all the warning she had before the door flew open.

Sam was never quiet when he came in from work. He stomped and banged things around as if the job had him set in a more aggressive mode. Everything was rougher and louder until he started to wind down.

But the sudden clatter in the formerly silent house startled her and she dropped the hardcover book she'd been shelving. The thump caught his attention.

He folded his arms over his chest, one eyebrow going right up as he looked from her to the open box on the floor. "Thought you were going to get this done before I came home?"

"I was. I mean I am—I'm almost done. It just took a little longer than I expected." She avoided meeting his gaze. It wasn't a lie. It just wasn't the whole truth. It took longer because she'd put it off for most of the day. She did have a reason, but she had a feeling that wasn't going to fly after so much procrastination.

"Charlie..." There was a warning tone in his voice.

She knew that tone and decided to give her excuse a shot. At this point it couldn't make things worse and it was a fairly decent reason to put things off; at least she thought so. She picked up the book she'd dropped and put it on the shelf. "I was looking over the online classes for the winter semester. I thought I'd see what was available. I mean, there's still the will to deal with."

She was referring to the codicil in her father's will that

said she had five years to get a doctorate, or else the ranch would remain under Sam's complete control permanently. If she wanted to be an equal partner she was going to have to put in the work.

Sam's mouth dropped open and for a second, he was speechless. "So... you decided to go ahead and do it then?"

"Doesn't seem like I have much choice." She sighed and stepped around the box to get to him; slipping into his arms was becoming an automatic reflex when she was upset. He had a way of soothing her. "I mean things are going great with us and we're working together fine, but it's just..."

He pulled her up close, wrapped his arms around her and rested his chin on her head. "Still bothers you that I have full control, huh?"

"Yeah—no, I dunno, Sam. It's weird. I gave you all kinds of power over me, even asked to skip the safewords so it would be more—*more*. And it's working out well. I'm happy to let you have total control of me. But when it comes to the ranch it's different. I feel like we should be equals, legally."

He was quiet and she worried she'd hurt his feelings. It was basically like saying she didn't trust him, and she did. "Sorry, Sam I know—"

He cut her off in mid-word. "You know there's the other option."

Another option? She shifted, tipping her head back so she could look into his eyes. "What do you mean?"

"Well, there was another codicil in the will. You get your doctorate or..." He let the words trail off.

Her eyes widened and the breath caught in her throat. The desire to run hit her hard as she struggled to breathe. She'd forgotten the other option. Forgotten it on purpose because she had trouble committing to any relationship, as Sam well knew.

"No!" The word burst from her so loud it startled them

both. She pulled out of his arms and closed her eyes, blocking him and everything else out as she tried to control the rising panic with breathing exercises her therapist had taught her.

He didn't touch her or try to talk. He'd learned by now that when she got like that, she just needed a minute, but he was there when she finally let out a long shuddering breath and opened her eyes.

"You okay, Darlin'?" He sounded so careful, like he was afraid she'd break.

She nodded, took another hitching breath. "I'm sorry, Sam. I didn't mean... it's not you. I love you. It's just..."

"I know baby. I get it. You've got commitment issues. We're working on it one day at a time, and you're getting better. Probably throwing the marriage thing at you wasn't the best idea. My fault; sorry, Charlie."

She looked up, checking him for signs of hurt and only when she saw his open expression could she relax. "You know if I were going to marry anyone, it would be you. You're the *only* one, Sam. Just not yet. Give me time."

He laughed and pulled her back into his arms. "All the time you need, Charlie. I'd love to put a ring on your finger but not until you're ready. And to be honest I'm not sure I'm ready for that either. I mean we just moved in together. We've got time for stuff like that later."

He always knew the right thing to say. There'd never been another man who knew her as well. She'd never let anyone else get close enough to know her as well as he did. And deep down some part of her had leapt at the idea of being his wife. There was a little girl inside who had once dreamed of long white dresses and forevers.

But there had been a lot of miles since those innocent childhood days and between then and now she'd changed. It was hard for her to accept that Sam would always be around, and that wasn't because of anything he'd ever done. It was all her and her own baggage.

"I love you, cowboy." She smiled up at him and then let herself melt back into his arms, surrendering to the warmth and safety they represented.

"I love you too, brat."

Emotional crisis averted, and bonus she'd totally distracted him from the fact that she hadn't finished unpacking. Or so she thought.

"So, do you want your spanking before dinner or after?" he asked.

Damn it.

CHAPTER 2

It was cute that she still thought she could get away with skirting around his orders. The fact that she'd been considering classes had thrown him, but he knew that hadn't taken her all day. Even if it had she'd been given a week to finish, so he had no sympathy for her.

She had a procrastination problem, but only when it came to doing things she didn't really want to do. It was something they were going to work on together. Well, she'd be working on it, and he'd be the one providing the motivation. Putting unpleasant things off never made them easier in the long run and she was more than old enough to know that.

He did give her some credit for getting most of it done. If she'd started just a little sooner, she probably would have saved herself a sore butt. Most of the place was looking a little less cluttered anyway, despite all the extra stuff she'd brought, and he appreciated that. But they would still be discussing it later.

He let it drop for the moment and went to shower off the sweat of a long day. He sighed when he saw that the bathroom was now crowded with dozens of bottles. He couldn't really complain since he'd been the one pushing her to unpack but he did grumble when he knocked a few of them into the tub.

He'd have to put up some shelves or something, so they weren't perched on every ledge. Not a big chore to get done, especially since they were going into the quiet part of the year. It was one more thing on his winter list.

The small foreman's house was just a temporary solution while the main house was being renovated anyway. Which reminded him to ask her how that was going. He took care of that during dinner. "You make those calls to the contractors today?" It was a casual question tossed out over dinner, but she was in a sulky mood since he'd made it clear she was still going to be punished.

She frowned and stabbed a piece of chicken a little harder than necessary. "No."

"Is this something else we're going to need to talk about, Charlie?" He put down his fork and leaned back in his chair. She didn't look up at him and had taken to pushing vegetables around her plate. He wondered if she knew that she looked exactly like a five-year-old who'd been told she couldn't have dessert.

"The contractors? No, I'll get it done. I just didn't have time today. I'm still putting together a list so I can get estimates in order."

He was sure she was on top of all that. She had a business management degree, and his Charlie was nothing if not professional when it came to organizing expenses. Shame it didn't transfer over to the rest of her life.

"Not the contractors, Charlie. The attitude."

She was silent, but he saw her sneaking looks at him, probably to see if she was close to getting herself in more trouble. She must have evaluated his expression and decided she better back it down because her next words were, "Sorry, Sam."

"You might as well call me Daddy because you're about to go over my knee, girl."

Every reaction was being weighed and judged and he made it clear with a piercing stare that had her shifting in her seat. "Sorry, Daddy."

He could almost hear the sigh she held back, and he had no doubt she would have rolled her eyes if he wasn't watching. It made his lip twitch and he had to fight not to show his amusement. He wouldn't have allowed any other signs of temper after the warning, but it did amuse him how dramatic she could be when she was being put in her place.

They were still working out the details of their relationship and most of the time everything seemed to settle naturally, but his Charlie never had liked being told what to do outside of the bedroom. Which, as far as he was concerned, made it all the more interesting that she'd asked for him to take charge of her.

Her asking him to boss her around had been confusing at first. It seemed so contrary to what he knew of her. He'd spent a lot of time wrapping his head around it and the conclusion he'd come to was that it felt more real to her if she didn't like it. That made sense and went along with her request to skip the safeword.

It had taken a bit to feel easy about that, but once he was sure it was what she really wanted he'd been perfectly willing to take their D/s out of the bedroom. He hadn't regretted it so far. Charlie was the girl for him. He'd known it since they were kids, and once he'd stepped into the role of Daddy it had been a perfect fit.

He was used to her bratty side; it made his palm itch to smack her ass until she behaved, but he loved her spirit too. In the bedroom when she slipped into the fiery submissive role it made his cock painfully hard. But he'd never seen the little girl in need of a Daddy until she'd come back to the ranch. It called out to him, and the Dom inside had answered eagerly.

It made him feel needed, important. It touched him on a level that was entirely different from the other parts of her. It could be sexy, but that was only the smallest piece of it. He'd never realized before he'd actually experienced it, but when she called him Daddy it made him feel like he was the center of her world.

Now he wasn't sure he could go back, not even if she decided she didn't want the dynamic anymore. When she'd arrived on his front step, soaked to the skin and clutching a stuffed toy, his heart had melted. Right then he'd claimed her as his babygirl, though he hadn't even known it until later.

But invoking the Daddy side of him came with consequences and if Charlie wasn't careful, she was going to feel them even if he had to interrupt dinner to do it. From the look on her face, she realized it and he could see her trying to move past the sulk. He helped her by changing the subject.

"So, made any decisions on what you're thinking of studying? Does it have to match your Masters, or can it be in anything?" He'd never gone to college, didn't have a degree, and had no clue about the academic path she was considering.

If he thought too hard about it sometimes it made him feel inadequate. She was smart as a whip, and there he was with just his high school diploma to see him through. Not that he needed anything more, but sometimes he wished he'd had the chance to go on with his education.

Maybe then he'd be more of a match for her intellectually. But it was just wishful thinking and most of the time he was content with who he was. Charlie was going to have enough education for both of them by the time she was through.

"Well, when I went for my other degrees, Jimmy refused to let me major in Animal Sciences, but now that he's gone, I think it's the smartest move, right?" She said it in a distracted tone like she wasn't really asking for his opinion, but he could see it wasn't that. She was afraid he'd discourage her like her father had.

He shrugged, giving her an easy grin to soothe her. "Makes sense to me. If this is the life you want there's no reason you shouldn't have it, Charlie. We've got a ranch to run so it seems like it could only help."

She relaxed visibly and a slight smile curved her lips. "That's what I was thinking. And honestly the business degree will go right along with it. I've got a ton of ideas for..." She trailed off and gave him an uncertain look.

From the sudden flush climbing her cheeks he knew she was recalling the fight they'd had when she tried to go around him to set up some of those plans. She'd come close to getting spanked on the spot over that one, and only the fact that they hadn't yet introduced punishment to the relationship had saved her.

Briefly. He'd taught her a few lessons about trying to take the reins already since then, and he had a feeling eventually she'd need more schooling on the issue.

One eyebrow went up as he gave her a stern look, but then he laughed and shook his head. "I'm always willing to listen to your ideas, Charlie. As long as you know who makes the final decisions around here." He speared a broccoli floret and chewed it thoughtfully before he continued.

"Listen, part of the problem with what you wanted to do was it wasn't going to work. You hadn't done the research. Plans are great but you need to back them up with facts and experience. If going to school is going to give you a better base for your ideas, I'm all for it."

She practically bounced in her seat. "Really? You promise you'll listen, really listen then?"

He held up one hand, three fingers raised. "I promise."

She snorted. "You were *never* a scout."

"Well, I promise anyway. Learn the trade, get some experience, and I'll listen. Besides, if you do go all the way and get your doctorate I'd have to listen because legally you'll have a say, right?"

She wiggled in her chair. "Yeah, technically, but I mean … you're Daddy now."

She looked so fucking adorable squirming, all full of embarrassment and determination. And she was right. Even if she ended up with a say legally, he'd still be in charge of *her*. At least he hoped so. So far, all signs were pointing to the relationship lasting.

They were both getting what they needed and that tended to go a long way towards keeping things intact. "And as your Daddy, I'm telling you that when you have a good idea, one that will work, I'll hear you and we'll give it a try. But you better have done your homework, or you might end up over my knee, little girl."

She rolled her eyes. "You wouldn't spank me for that, Daddy."

"Wouldn't I? Try me." But the smirk on his face said he was teasing her and once she saw that she laughed. There probably would be a spanking if she brought him another unlikely idea, but it would be because she threw a fit when he pointed out why it wouldn't work.

He knew his Charlie and she struggled with the word no.

But the banter had done what he'd intended, and the pouting was done. They chatted over the remains of the meal. When she brought out a fresh blueberry pie for dessert, he pulled her into his lap and insisted on feeding her a slice one bite at a time.

She was giggling and happy by the time they finished eating, but there was still something he had to take care of. It wasn't going to be a severe punishment, but she needed something to remind her not to put things off until the last minute. Once there was nothing left but the purple juice and crumbs on their plate, he reminded her that she was owed a punishment.

There was an immediate reaction. "Oh no, Daddy! Please, I was almost done." Her bottom lip quivered, and her eyes had gone wide and pleading.

"Almost doesn't cut it, Charlie. Not when you had weeks to do this," he said, shaking his head.

"But..."

"Nope. You're going over my knee, but if you don't fuss about it too much it'll just be my hand this time. You need to learn that putting off unpleasant things doesn't make them go away, kiddo."

She sighed and pressed her face into his neck. "I want them to go away though."

"Uh-huh. I know. But since it ain't gonna happen, we need to go ahead and do the hard things anyway, right?" He kept his voice low and gentle, as he rubbed slow circles on her back.

"I guess." She drew the words out mournfully.

"Right. So, I want you to go to the corner. That one over there," He gestured to the empty spot in the far corner of the main room. Despite the clutter in the small cabin, he'd insisted it stay open just for her. "-and think about how you're going to do things different next time."

She didn't like the corner. Spankings, even if they were punishment, she could sometimes enjoy if they weren't too heavy, but it was these little additions that put her head in the right place for being punished. It took it out of the sexy category and made it real discipline, which was what she needed and wanted, despite her reluctance.

She made a soft whining sound, but he ignored it and set her on her feet. "Now, Charlie."

She went, dragging her feet and moving as slowly as she could get away with. He gave her a moment once she was settled there and then cleared his throat. It was a reminder, and she knew exactly what she was supposed to do.

She liked to act as if she'd forgotten every time, but now with a sigh she pushed her baggy sweatpants and underwear down to her knees.

"Shirt too, little girl. You know better by now. I'm going to start doubling your punishment if you keep pretending like you don't know what to do in the corner." The words were cool, with an edge of sternness that said he was close to making that decision.

She quickly pulled up her t-shirt and tucked it around her waist so that her ass was bare.

"Better." He knew that was one of the hardest parts for her to get through. Baring her own ass made her an active participant in her punishment. It engaged her mind and her emotions in what was happening—but of course it was also embarrassing.

It was meant to be.

He let her stand there, shuffling and mumbling under her breath for about ten minutes before he said a word. He enjoyed watching her in the corner. She would shoot him shy looks, trying to see what he was doing, but each time her eyes met his and she'd quickly turn back.

They'd talked about the corner time rules. He'd made it clear what he expected of her, and eventually he'd tighten the reins a little more and start punishing her for those small lapses. At the moment though, he just found it amusing that she always thought she could get away with it, as if he wasn't sitting right here watching.

"You let me know when you're ready for your spanking, Charlie." She hated that, and he knew it. It was another way to make her take part in her own discipline. He felt like it was important that she wasn't always passive when it came to these things. He could and did grab and spank when she was having a fit. She quickly regretted pushing him to that point when the fast flurry of spanks heated her ass up to scorching.

But sometimes it was necessary that she be reminded she'd asked for this, that she was an equal participant in this relationship. It was too easy to sink into the mindset that this was being done to her instead of *for* her that way.

So, sometimes he dropped the ball in her lap to force her to make choices in her own punishment. Now she'd have to struggle with the decision—stand there longer, with her bare ass hanging out, or go ahead and say she was ready. The latter would then cause the spanking she was trying to avoid.

Maybe it was mean. He was pretty sure *she* thought it was. He could hear her grumbling about it under her breath at that very moment, but he also thought it was good for her.

Besides, he liked to make private bets with himself on how long she'd hold out before finally giving in. Charlie was stubborn.

But then so was he.

CHAPTER 3

She really had thought he was going to let the packing slide. She should have known better. Sam didn't like changing his mind, even when she was mad at him. Then they'd had dinner, and eventually she'd realized pouting wasn't going to do any good, so she'd given it up. Besides, she liked their homey little meals together. It was so domestic and relaxing to catch up on the news of the day while they ate.

The food had even been decent. The chicken was a little dry because she'd overcooked it by a few minutes while distracted with the boxes, but it had been passable. The pie had been excellent, and more than made up for it anyway. She couldn't take the credit for that though. It came from the market stand a mile down the road and they never disappointed.

She shouldn't have been surprised by his support. Sam had always encouraged her to do whatever made her happy … as long as it didn't involve driving him insane. It was her father who had always been stuck on her doing something unrelated to the ranching life.

For a man who'd loved the family spread with all his heart, he'd had a confusing amount of trouble understanding that his daughter felt the same. He'd decided she was too good for such a rough life and that was that.

So now she had a Master's in business that she didn't really want, but if she could use that to complete a doctorate in animal sciences it would be worth it. And she could use both degrees to really put a shine on the old place.

She could see herself and Sam running the place together then. Partners. She didn't hate the idea, though the fact that she'd nearly had a full-blown panic attack when he'd mentioned a different kind of partnership told her she still had some work to do on her relationship issues.

She'd deliberately put that ridiculously old-fashioned codicil out of her head for a reason. There was no way she was marrying Sam to skip ahead and get her share of the ranch. She resented having to slog her way through a degree to get there, but at least that would be through her own hard work and not because of catering to some ridiculous medieval clause.

If—*when* she married Sam it would be because she was ready and wanted to. Someday she'd be there, maybe not any time soon, but someday.

Sitting in his lap as he fed her pie had gone a long way towards soothing those frayed nerves. She'd been relaxed and happy right up until he'd reminded her about the punishment and sent her to the corner. She sighed and kicked the wall with her toe, frustrated and embarrassed to be standing there with her pants down.

She snuck a look back over her shoulder as she fidgeted and waited for it to be done, but he caught her immediately. She muttered something rude about him under her breath as she snapped back around. She had an active mind and standing there staring at the wall was torture. Well, maybe not torture exactly, but she hated it.

Why couldn't he just spank her and get it over with?

She knew the answer to that, of course, but that didn't stop her from being annoyed about it. The Daddy thing had settled into their relationship and although it had thrown her in the beginning, she'd really come around. But it had since grown beyond a sexy bedroom thing. Sam had a strong Daddy Dom side. He'd been trying to take care of her since they were both kids, and now she'd given him license to be the boss full time.

Part of putting him in charge had been accepting that punishments that weren't fun would come along with it. She'd been prepared for that. What she hadn't expected was how *young* some of them would make her feel. The embarrassment, the knowing what was about to happen, they combined to give her this nervous little girl feeling that she had trouble shaking off.

She'd never really understood the DD/lg dynamic, but the simple Daddy kink had grown into something closer to that kind of relationship when they'd started playing again. In the beginning calling him Daddy had felt weird and awkward, but now it felt normal.

At times with the punishment and caretaking, it felt more parental, and she was surprisingly okay with that because it came with a feeling of being safe and secure in his arms. She liked being taken care of and spoiled a little bit. It was the humiliating punishments she didn't like.

Well, at least she told herself she didn't like them. She was far too aware of the very different feelings under the surface. Sometimes those punishments were a turn on, sometimes the embarrassment factor added to that to make her wet and needy for his touch. But aside from that there was something cathartic about a punishment that pulled up a whole range of emotions.

It started with nervousness, dread, frustration, and even anger. Then once they moved onto the spanking part of the cycle it became sadness, regret, guilt, sometimes there was still lingering frustration. It could take a while to get past it sometimes, but then, finally, there wasn't room for any of that. There was just the pain and the tears until it was over.

The best part came once they were finished with all of that. The part when he soothed her and made her know she was forgiven. Then she felt like his good girl again and could let go of the guilt and self-critical thoughts and just be his as he wrapped her in his arms and rocked her.

It was worth all of the rest of the cycle but remembering that as she stood there waiting could be hard sometimes.

His voice came out of nowhere, sounding loud in the silent room. "You let me know when you're ready for your spanking, Charlie."

She'd known that was coming, but it had the same effect as always. Two seconds before she'd been bored to death and ready to get out, but as soon as he said that she changed her mind. Stubborn determination set in and she remained there, silently glaring at the wall in front of her.

She shifted from one foot to the other and counted the cracks in the wooden planks in front of her to kill the time. Every time she thought about telling him she was ready, her butt would start to tingle and tense, and she'd put it off for another minute or so. But that could only go on so long and the night was passing.

She knew that Sam wouldn't budge until she did what he wanted. She also knew that morning came early on the ranch; if she wanted any chance for a little fun after the punishment she had to give in before it got too late. Punishment, before it started and once it was over, tended to arouse her. And like getting a lollipop after a shot, sex could soothe the sting.

Usually Sam refused to allow her pleasure after a punishment; he thought it blurred the lines too much. But she had a feeling he'd bend on this one. He was just using his hand and that meant he wasn't too mad about things. It was pretty obvious she'd made an attempt to obey even if she hadn't quite finished, so he'd probably decided to be lenient with her.

With that in mind she let out a long, overly dramatic sigh, and turned around. "I'm ready."

"You sure you don't want to stand there another ten minutes and break your record?" He looked amused, sitting back in his chair with his legs sprawled out in front of him and his arms crossed over his chest.

She scowled, but when she spoke, she was careful to keep her tone polite. "No, thank you. I'd like to get it over with so we can get on with our night. I'd like to spend a little time not being punished before you have to go to bed." She let a little bit of seduction creep into her voice.

He knew exactly what she was hoping for, she could tell by the way the amusement vanished and he sat up straight, patting his leg for her to come and lay across his lap.

"Let's get this over with then."

She didn't bother to pull up her pants. Instead, she kicked them off, along with her panties, and walked over to him in just the t-shirt. She stopped right in front of him, hesitating. There was always that moment just before punishment when she wondered why she wanted to live like this. A flash of *Are you out of your mind? You don't really want this.* would go through her head.

It never lasted, just a few moments of panic when she realized she was about to be spanked. It was always followed by a moment of clarity. She knew exactly why she wanted, needed, this life. It wasn't because she couldn't manage herself like any adult. It wasn't because she was too immature to get things done. It was because submitting to him unlocked things deep inside and set them free.

Being spanked uncaged her emotions. She needed the catharsis the pain brought. But it wasn't only that. It was Sam. He took her to places she couldn't go on her own. Everything about the way he dominated her made her feel alive. Her body trembled just thinking about his hands all over her.

Those rough, workingman hands that caressed her skin and brought pleasure when she behaved. When she was a bad girl, they brought a searing burn that made her regret displeasing him. But it was the way he held her, like she was the most precious thing in his life, like she was his sole focus, that she loved the most.

The rules and structure were good for her, she thought. Sam kept her from slacking off on things she'd rather not deal with and she liked that. It was *useful*, but their relationship was about more than that. He gave the orders; she followed them... or chose not to. Both choices brought them close with an intensity that took her breath away.

The moment passed and with it the panic. She lowered herself across his knees and stretched out with her hands flat on the floor. They wouldn't stay there, but for now she was the perfect picture of an obedient little girl about to be punished.

The spanking didn't begin immediately. He rubbed her bare cheeks, slowly at first and then briskly like he was preparing her skin for what was coming. When the first slap came it was almost anticlimactic, only the faintest sting which vanished quickly. It was little more than a pat.

It surprised her. He didn't usually do warm-ups when she was in trouble. She almost looked back over her shoulder to see what was going on, but then his hand came down again, just a little harder. "So, this problem you had with getting the unpacking done... was it because you're still having doubts about our relationship, Charlie?"

Now she understood why he was starting slow. He wanted to talk. A fast flurry of smacks didn't tend to be conducive to thinking so that made sense. But for once she could give him the answer he wanted. "No, no Daddy. No doubts about us. I promise."

"You sure?" His fingers lightly stroked across her skin, trailing along the seam of her ass. "No worrying that this won't work out? Nothing like that?"

She twisted, looking back over her shoulder so he could see her face. "No Daddy. Actually, things have been going ... good. Better than I expected."

Tension she hadn't realized he was holding drained from him. She could see his shoulders softening and the lines in his forehead smoothed out. "So, this was just the usual avoiding things you don't want to do?"

"Yes Daddy... um mostly it was indecision. I was having trouble deciding what I needed for the next few months we're here. There's not exactly a ton of extra room and I know you don't like the clutter, so I was waffling on decisions." It really was that simple. No deep emotional secrets this time. Just her not wanting to decide.

"Good. Then let's just make sure you have good motivation to figure things out faster next time," he said. He timed his hand to come down just as he said the last word.

She was watching, so she knew it was coming but it landed hard and she couldn't help but jump. "Ow! It doesn't have to be so hard," she said, whining.

"Yeah, it does." There was no more slow build. His hand began to fall fast, and every time it came down with a fierce sting. By the tenth smack she was wiggling and kicking her legs.

"I'm sorry, Daddy! I tried to get it done before you came home. I only needed a few more minutes." Her tone was frantic, and her voice rose in pitch as the barrage of spanks continued to cover every inch of her ass with blotches of heat and pain. Her thighs weren't exempt either. As soon as she started to kick her legs up, he turned his attention there. He slapped the meaty part of her upper legs a few times in a row until her feet hit the floor and stayed there.

As soon as they went down, he resumed spanking her ass. It was a clear warning, and she got the point. Her hands had left the floor; one was now wrapped around his ankle and the other was swingingly uselessly in the air... but she was careful not to try to block the crisp smacks that rained down.

This was punishment and she wasn't supposed to like it, she reminded herself as it got increasingly harder to stay still. Knowing that logically didn't do a damn thing to help deal with all the searing handprints he was landing across her backside though.

She wasn't anywhere near tears, there wasn't enough emotion involved to call them up this time. That didn't stop her from making plenty of noise. She'd learned early on that it was better not to be stoic. It wasn't just because Sam would take it as a sign that she needed extra. It was also better for her emotional state.

Every few spanks a yelp, or some variation of 'Ow, that hurts!' would burst from her. She could get exceedingly dramatic and loud at times, and every time he spanked her, she felt a surge of gratitude that there was no one within hearing distance.

She could let herself be loud without worrying anyone would hear because there was no one around for miles. It seemed to help her get through it. She could have held it all back, covered her mouth, and taken the spanking quietly, but what would be the point of that. Muffling her reactions just tended to make her shut down. It was as if refusing to express the pain made it harder to connect to it.

Not with the physical pain. She couldn't have avoided feeling that if she tried. But whenever she stubbornly refused to be vocal, she had trouble feeling all the emotions she was supposed to feel during a spanking. Afterwards, instead of the catharsis and then that state of blissful emptiness… she just ended up feeling frustrated.

It wasn't very flattering, but the only way she could describe it was like being a clogged sink. She needed all the emotions to pour through her, otherwise she got stuck and everything just sat there. For her being stuck meant she tended to antagonize Sam until he punished her again, harder.

It was better just to yelp and howl the first time—and she did a lot of it as he peppered her rump for a good five minutes. It seemed like far longer, and she kept checking to make sure the old clicking clock on the wall hadn't stopped.

There was a prickle of tears at the back of her eyes, but none had escaped. It wasn't a surprise. Tears tended to come when she actually felt bad about what she'd done. Sometimes she could get there from pain alone, but it usually had to be a much longer spanking.

There was a pulse in the center of each sore cheek to prove it had been a thorough spanking even if it hadn't lasted too long. Her thighs were stinging too, and she knew if she looked in the mirror, she'd see a whole lot of red blotches coating her skin.

It took her a few seconds, once he stopped, to be sure the spanking was over. She relaxed then, letting her body go boneless as she sprawled across his thighs. This was the part she liked. After the spanking, when everything was still fiery and hot, but she could stop trying to anticipate the next smack and just lie there and let her mind drift.

If it had been a more severe spanking, he probably wouldn't have rubbed some of the sting away after. But when he began to soothe the prickling heat with gentle caresses, she upped her chances for turning things to a more fun direction. The places he'd just spanked were close to other more *intimate* areas, and before long his fingers had trailed down the crease to where her thighs were held tightly together.

He didn't press in, just gently tickled along the line until she eased her legs apart in subtle invitation. He ignored that and continued to skirt the edges. So near and yet so far from where she wanted his fingers. Just the close proximity of his hand excited her. There was a tickle as arousal began to soak the short thatch of dark curls that covered her sex.

Her ass still smarted, but the sting was starting to sink in, becoming a more pleasant sensation that she could enjoy. He began to scratch his fingernails across the sensitized skin, drawing little designs over her flesh. It tickled, but in a sexy way. She couldn't stop the moan that escaped.

She inched her legs a little farther apart, lifting her ass. The invitation was more blatant now, practically demanding. He laughed.

"Something you want there, babygirl?"

Torn between frustration and need she didn't hold back the whimper. "I want you, Daddy."

"And what do you want from me, Charlie? You want more spanking?"

Her ass clenched automatically at the thought. "No, no I've had enough spanking," she assured him emphatically. It wasn't quite true. Now that the burning had settled in and was less intense, the idea of a nicer, more sensual spanking wasn't unappealing.

"You sure?"

"Yes…"

"Positive?" There was a teasing tone there. He knew she was conflicted somehow.

"Well… maybe a little more spanking would be okay. A not-punishment spanking," she hastened to add.

His fingers played along the crack of her ass and then suddenly his hand came down hard on her left cheek. She gasped, bucking up wildly in surprise. She hadn't expected a hard one.

He dropped his voice low, almost growling, "Spankings that aren't punishment can still hurt, Charlie. What would you say if I wanted to spank you without mercy, until you screamed and begged? And it would be for no reason at all, except that I wanted to?"

Her pussy clenched hard, a sudden torrent of arousal gushed and began to run down her inner thighs. Why was that *so* hot? Just thinking about it was enough to make her clit spasm. "I guess I'd say, 'yes Daddy'."

He chuckled and the low, liquid sound of amusement seemed to stroke her most intimate places. And then he finally slid his hand between her thighs to cup and squeeze her soaked folds with a possessive hand. She pushed into it, making a small needy sound.

"Good girl. That's the right answer." Slowly one of his fingers pressed in, separating her lower lips until it was nestled between them. He began to tap her clit with the tip of one finger and she writhed desperately needing more.

She trembled with the need to roll her hips to get more than just the tapping which was nothing but a tease. "Please, please I need…" The words trailed off into pleading whimpers. She wanted the harsh spanking he dangled in front of her like a treat, but she also wanted him to finger her until she came. The frustration was because he wasn't doing either.

"Oh, I know what you need, Charlie. But this did start out as punishment so I'm not entirely sure I should just give it you. Maybe there should be a cost involved so I know that you can separate punishment from fun."

She couldn't hold back anymore, and she began to move her hips, trying to get some friction against her throbbing clit. He stopped tapping and instead pressed his finger on the spot firmly. She wondered if he could feel the pulsing. It certainly seemed to echo through her whole body.

"A… cost? What kind of cost?" He was playing games with her. It could be fun, but it could also drive her crazy.

His finger moved, sliding in a slow circle around the hard little nub. She gasped, rocking back for more, but there was no more. He took his hand away and she let out a long, frustrated moan.

"Hmm. Seems like since you're the one who got in trouble, and I'm the one who had to do all the work of spanking your stubborn butt… I should be the one getting to feel good. Don't you think?" Her mouth opened but before she could answer his hand slapped down hard. It stayed where it landed. He squeezed the sore cheek and jiggled it in his grip.

She hissed in a breath between her teeth. What he was doing was reigniting all the sting from the earlier spanking and that made it hard to think. "I—that does sound fair." She knew it was the only appropriate answer. But she actually enjoyed it when he made her get down on her knees and take his cock into her mouth. That level of submission was sexy as hell.

He let go of her and she slid back off his lap, kneeling at his side and looking up at him. He made her hungry, but not for food. She wanted everything from him. Every touch, every kiss, every moment of time... all of it. She licked her lips in that slow, deliberately sexy way that made him hard.

"What do you want me to do, *Daddy*?" There was a purr to the word now.

The way she called him Daddy when she was trying to be sexy was vastly different from how she did it when she was in trouble. She'd learned to enjoy the taste of it in her mouth. Now each time she called him that, she was reminded that he loved her. She no longer needed to be coaxed to say it, except when she was feeling stubborn.

"I want you to use your mouth, Charlie. Now, and if you do a good job *maybe* I'll let you come afterwards. Or maybe I'll just go ahead and give you that merciless spanking. I guess it depends on how good you are." There was no *almost* in his voice now, it was all sexy growl and it pulled at her, demanding her obedience.

And she wanted to be obedient. She kept her eyes on him, their gazes locked as she moved around in front. She pressed her hand to the front of his baggy pajama bottoms, tracing the heavy shaft and then gripping it through the material. It jumped, tenting the soft fabric.

She pushed her hand down under the loose waistband to hold the hot length of him, and then after some fumbling, she freed it from its confines. It was hard and heavy in her hand.

She watched the expression on his face as she wrapped her fingers around his erection and began to pump slowly up and down. She had in mind a long tease. It was only fair, that was what he'd been doing to her. But Sam had other ideas and he allowed her only a minute or two of slow stroking before one eyebrow went up.

"That your way of saying you don't want to come tonight, girl?" There was no anger in his voice, no sign that he was having any emotion about her playing with him at all. There was just that firm warning that she was risking what she wanted most.

"Why would you say that?" She widened her eyes and tried to look confused.

"I said use your mouth. And if you're talking then your mouth obviously isn't full, now is it?"

Her bottom lip curled out and she sighed. "I was getting to it... I thought you liked starting off slow?"

His eyes narrowed. "Not seeing too many orgasms in your future, Charlie. Might want to rethink where you're going with this."

That did put things into a different perspective, and she decided to quit while she was ahead. She dropped her gaze to his lap and went to work. First, she used her tongue, licking like he was the most delicious candy she'd ever tasted, but when his hips begin to lift out of the seat, demanding more, she let her mouth slide over the head.

At first, she just held him there, teasing around the underside with the tip of her tongue. That was where most of the nerve endings were and he groaned as his hand fisted in her hair. The sound was loud in the quiet room.

She pulled him deeper inch by inch, moving slowly to caress and excite as she did. By the time she'd taken as much of him as her mouth could hold, he was prodding at the back of her throat. She settled her hands on his hips and began to bob her head, slowly at first, just getting a feel.

There was so much tension in his body as he fought the urge to fuck her mouth. He'd done that before and some-thing about the way she gagged on the length of him drove him crazy, but it was something she needed prep to handle and he knew that.

She appreciated that he held himself back and let her go at her own pace. He was good about remembering her limits during sex, especially when they added in a little kink as they usually did.

While she'd chosen not to have safewords for punishment, they did use them for play, and she'd learned that even during sex they could be useful to keep things on the same page. When things got a little rough, and especially when Sam brought in the ropes, a quick 'yellow' could give her the seconds she needed to catch up to him.

She'd even used 'red' a few times when something had felt wrong, but in those cases, she usually found that Sam was already stopping to check on her before she even got the word out. He seemed attuned to her in some ways, hyperaware of her body and her reactions. When a rope twisted and her arms started to go numb, he'd been there loosening them almost before she'd noticed herself.

He was equally attentive outside of the bedroom and when things got serious, they'd sat down together to work out her limits. When she said that she loved a *little* bit of choking on his cock, but only with advance warning, he stuck with that. But oh, she could feel how desperately he wanted to thrust deep from the tension and the way he held his hips so still.

She dug her fingers into his thighs and began to move her head, hollowing her cheeks to give that extra bit of suck that he loved. She didn't want to have to fight her gag reflex, so she didn't try to deep-throat him. She liked the idea of it more than she actually liked doing it and Sam honestly didn't seem to care as long as her mouth was on him.

With quick shallow movements she brought him close to the edge. She could hear his ragged breathing and knew he wasn't going to last much longer. But before he got there, he tugged at her hair and pulled her back. "Stop."

She let his cock slide from her mouth with a little pop and looked up surprised. "You don't want…"

"Nope, not yet. I've got a surprise for you." He pushed the chair back and stood up, holding out a hand to help her up. Then, with a smack to the ass he sent her towards the bedroom. She laughed as she sprawled on the bed and waited for him to join her, but he made a quick stop first.

She watched, her whole body humming with excitement.

One of them needed to come soon or she was going to explode. A surprise though... that could be good or bad depending on his mood. Either way it was exciting.

CHAPTER 4

Now that she was his again and things had finally settled into a stable relationship, he sometimes had to hold himself back. Like a kid in a candy store he wanted to try everything. He wanted the stuff they'd already done and enjoyed, but also all of those exciting little games he'd planned but never had an outlet for.

They crowded in his mind and he pictured what it would be like to actually play them out with her. It was just starting to become less frantic and more relaxed between them. She was learning to accept the punishment aspect of the relationship she'd asked for, and she broke the rules less. Which meant they had time for more play.

While tonight had started with punishment, she hadn't been especially naughty this time, and he saw no reason to dump the plans he'd made now that he'd corrected her mistake. But he did feel like she needed to pay for her share of the pleasure that was coming, just to make sure she did separate punishment from fun.

It also gave him an excuse to indulge in one of his favorite things: her mouth on his cock. She wouldn't just be making up for her procrastination with a blow job though. He had an exciting little twist that would fit perfectly. It was something they had done once before, and he'd never forgotten how amazing it had been. It had figured heavily in his masturbation fantasies for years.

Oh yeah, this is going to be great. In the bedroom, he took a minute to dig around in a drawer. He pulled out a toy he'd had for a long time and swished it through the air. "Remember this, Darlin'?"

She squinted and then her eyes widened. "Oh, I do!" There was a mixture of excited anticipation and concern there. No doubt she was wondering if he'd decided to punish her more. A birch could be fearsome when used harshly, and this was similar, but he didn't intend to be mean. The look on his face must have given her a clue.

He swished the implement through the air. It was long and flexible, basically a synthetic version of a birch. All the sting but without the mess of wood splinters to clean up after. He liked it because it was the perfect length to use on her while she had her mouth on him. Best of both worlds.

He knew exactly when she put two and two together and figured out what he had in mind because a slow grin spread across her lips.

She tilted her head, giving him an innocent look. "You think I need some encouraging, Daddy?" There was a purr to the word 'Daddy' and when she said it like that it made his cock jerk. There was nothing little-girlish about it in that moment.

"Couldn't hurt. Sometimes I just don't think you put your best effort into things, Charlie." It was a struggle not to grin along with her. Instead, he tossed the birch onto the bed and stripped out of his clothes.

He got comfortable on his back, head on the pillows, and motioned for her to move over to his left side. She settled there on her hands and knees, ass wiggling teasingly as she leaned down to lick at his hard shaft. Her hair shielded her face like a dark curtain, and he reached out to tuck it back behind her ears. He wanted to see her expressions during this.

He wanted to watch as she took him into her mouth. But she was back to teasing, taunting him to use the birch as she hinted at the pleasures waiting for him. She got comfortable, spread her knees wide for balance and lowered herself to her elbows as she tasted and licked. Her mouth would dip over the head of his shaft but then she'd let it slip free.

He knew what she wanted. He picked up the birch and snapped it across her bare ass and thighs. Since his erection was in no danger from her teeth, he didn't bother to be gentle and it was a hard stroke.

She jumped with a gasp, and gave him a pouting look, but it got the message across. When she leaned back in, she took him in her mouth and began to suck.

The short break had given him a little more endurance, but he knew it wouldn't take long to bring him to the edge. Her tongue stroked him as her head bobbed, taking his length deeper each time. The wet heat felt like home and he groaned as his head fell back. For a second, he just let himself enjoy the way her mouth collapsed around his erection, so the wet heat hugged the shaft.

He hadn't gotten out the birch for nothing. Once he'd adjusted enough to catch his breath, he began to use it. It was gentler than before, but enough to sting. He could encourage her towards what he liked that way, and did, though there wasn't much about a blow job that he didn't like.

It wasn't all that different from having sex, except that it was more intense in ways he couldn't entirely explain. Her mouth was more reactive, adapting to his movements as his hips slowly rocked upwards. She had a little more control this way, which was why there was nothing quite like being sucked off.

But there was more to it than that. With all the work on her side he could lay back and let himself drift into the sensations. Swinging the birch occasionally was no effort at all and getting to enjoy the look on her face as she concentrated on his cock heightened everything for him.

It made it hard to focus, especially when he was so close, but he enjoyed watching the way she gave the task all her focus. Her eyes closed as she immersed herself in the act of lavishing attention on his cock. The birch swung slow and steady, encouragement but no unexpected pain while he was nestled so vulnerably between her teeth.

It was just enough burn to keep her going and each time it whooshed across her ass she'd put a little more enthusiasm into what she was doing. It was like a reward for spanking her, and he loved it. It took effort to keep from increasing the speed and force of each strike just to get to the end, but he wanted to draw it out as long as possible.

"Fuck, Charlie… if you always used your mouth like *this* you'd never get in trouble." The growled words seemed barely human.

She made a sound of garbled laughter, and the feel of it around the head of his cock made his balls tighten. Tension ran the length of his body as he tried to hold out, but it was too much. There was the usual pushing/pulling inside as his body hurtled desperately towards orgasm. His cock demanded to come, while his mind tried to pull it back to make the goodness continue just a *little* longer. It was always a losing battle.

There was a gathering sensation in his middle, a feeling of everything being pulled to the center. He barely had time to warn her before his hips bucked and then he was emptying himself into her mouth one jerk at a time. Her rapid swallowing drew out the pleasure for an endless moment while he hovered there.

He heard a shout and realized it was his. His breath sounded loud and ragged in his own ears. And her throat gagging around the tip as she tried to swallow down every drop suddenly shifted from wonderful to way-too-sensitive and it balanced on being so good it actually hurt.

For a second, he understood her desire for pain mixed with pleasure, because that endless torment as her mouth worked at his overly sensitive cock was both. It hit a threshold where he could no longer stand it, and he reached out to bury his hand in her hair, dragging her back.

She resisted at first, then slowly let him slide from her mouth but even that was intense. The feel of her teeth lightly grazing along the still semi-hard shaft had his hands clenching the sheets as his ass left the bed. Then he was free, and he slumped back down. A loud whoosh of air left his lungs with an explosive curse at the end.

She wiped her mouth on the back of her hand with a ladylike primness and gave him a smug look. "Well, Daddy, was I a good girl?" She looked so pleased with herself that he couldn't resist snapping the birch across the middle of her thighs one more time. She yelped and sat back on her heels quickly to protect her ass.

He made it good and hard on purpose; it was his turn to look smug. "Hell yeah, you were." He stopped to clear his raspy throat. The shouting had made it rough. "You did such a good job that you're going to have to give me a minute to recover though."

A look of consternation crossed her face as she realized that he was in no shape to give her the immediate pleasure she needed so badly. He let her think that for a second before he offered her the solution he'd decided on in advance.

"Of course, if you come sit on my face ... I imagine I have

enough energy to handle that." There was a little teasing to the tone, but there was a hungry edge there too. He wanted to taste her. Wanted to feel her dancing against his lips as he drove his tongue into her.

It was one position Charlie was shy about. She seemed to feel that she might be too heavy, or that he wouldn't be able to breathe under her. But she was wound tight enough now that he thought she might be able to get beyond that.

He was right. She was eager enough, and after changing positions, she eased herself down over his mouth. The way she kept checking to make sure he was okay was adorable. But the third time she tried to get up, he gripped her hips in both hands, dragged her back down and held her there so he could explore her dripping heat.

There was something so satisfying about driving her to lose control until she forgot to be worried about him or the fact that she was straddling his face. He kept her there as he swept his tongue through the slippery folds, stroking and teasing until he found her clit.

She was perfectly positioned for him to lavish the hard little nub with attention and he did so with enthusiasm; her loud moans and gasps could be heard even with her thighs covering his ears. It was almost enough to make him hard all over again and his cock twitched and stirred valiantly.

It was harder to hold her in place when he was putting all his effort into licking and sucking her clit. Her hips rolled until she was grinding down against his tongue and he buried his mouth between the spread pussy lips to lap up the flowing juices.

He wanted to devour her, wanted to drive her over the edge until she screamed his name, and he wasn't going to be satisfied by anything less. He drove her there and it didn't take long. When she finally came his name echoed through the room. Only then did he let her roll off of him, panting and whimpering with sensory overload. His face glistened with her juices. He settled back feeling pleased and satisfied with himself and pulled her trembling body up against his.

It was a good night, one of the best he could remember. The memory of her entire body shuddering and shaking as she rode his face and came against his tongue over and over would be locked in his mind forever. His jaw ached and his tongue had a cramp in it, but it had all been worth it to push her past the edge of control.

"You look so fucking beautiful when you ride my face," he said.

She let out a breathy snort. "You couldn't even see anything!"

"Didn't need to. I just know." He sounded so smug and pleased about it, that it made her burst out laughing. It was the perfect end to his day.

CHAPTER 5

She was the best kind of sore in the morning. Every stretch brought back memories of the night before and it left her smiling as she went about her day. The final box was easily taken care of, and then Charlie settled herself down to deal with the appraisals on the big house. The figures were daunting for a girl who'd never felt like there was a lot of extra money around.

When she thought back, she realized how privileged she'd been growing up. She knew her father had wanted it that way. He gave her everything she needed but kept her from being spoiled by making her work for it.

No one sat around on a ranch, there was just too much to do, but she'd had what she needed and a lot of things she wanted too. In her head she'd always pictured her father scrimping for those things. The fact that he'd made her do extra chores and save her money to pay for at least part of what she wanted had equated to the idea that money was tight.

It was only after his death that she'd discovered how wrong she was about the financial situation. Graduating college and then getting a master's degree without having to burden herself with a lot of student loans should have been a big clue that they weren't broke. She'd just been too busy being mad that he was forcing her to go to school at all, to think about where the money had come from.

Having to take out loans would have given her an excuse to say no to the whole thing, so Jimmy hadn't even put the suggestion on the table. He'd simply paid for it. It was probably the only thing he'd ever paid for outright without making her kick in at least a pittance so she would feel like she'd earned it.

Now he was gone, and she'd been stunned to learn he'd left her quite a bit of money in investments. That wasn't the biggest shock she'd received at the reading of his will, of course. His decision to put the ranch in her ex's hands, leaving him half of the property and full control until Charlie got her Doctorate had been a bitter pill to swallow. She was still struggling to deal with how she felt about it.

But things were getting easier over time. Her fears and baggage were slowly diminishing as she saw her relationship with Sam become more stable. Maybe eventually marriage would actually be an option for her. It was just that every time she considered the idea, she saw her mother walking out the door and never coming back.

Therapy had helped, but it never really went away. After so many years there should have been some kind of closure, but it remained an open wound. She'd been willing to accept that it would always be a painful hole that could never be sealed over, but recently she'd changed her mind on that. She wanted to get over it and now she had good reason to try harder.

In the meantime, she was hoping that doing some major renovations on the house she'd grown up in would help to wipe away some of the memories. There had been dark times in that house, things she didn't like to think about. Her mother and father had fought with each other constantly until one day her mother had walked out and never come back. But aside from that, most of the memories were actually good.

She'd had a very happy childhood with her father, but now the good memories were just as hard to live with as the dark ones. Constantly being reminded of his booming laugh, the scent of his aftershave, and the horrible western music he blasted when he cooked breakfast in the mornings kept the grief fresh.

Moving in with Sam had been smart. It was cramped and they got on each other's nerves occasionally, but it had immediately lifted her mood and made it easier to get through the days. The plan she was working towards was to change the main house completely so that it would purge the memories and then they'd both move over where there was enough room and space.

So far there hadn't been much progress towards that goal. But despite the fact that Sam had let her off easily in the punishment department the night before, she *had* taken his lecture to heart. Putting off difficult things didn't make them go away, so it was time to make some decisions.

There were three estimates sitting in front of her right now, and she was finally taking the time to go through them. The prices varied wildly, based on the options they'd offered her, but all of them seemed reasonable. The timelines on each one felt less optimal since, depending on her choices, they could be looking at a finish date of six months to a year down the road.

As much as she loved Sam's homey little cabin, she couldn't really see living in it for most of a year. Charlie had always been someone who needed her own space to decompress. Living with him was great but the cabin was essentially two rooms and a bath, which meant she didn't really have any place to be by herself when he was home.

If she did decide to go back to school that was going to be a bigger problem. She needed an office where she could lock herself away to work, but she'd sort that out later. Sighing, she sat back and frowned. There were too many choices to make and she'd never been great at making big decisions when there were so many options. She needed to narrow them down.

"Need versus want, Charlie," she said under her breath. She continued to cheer herself on mentally as she made lists, and then crossed things off them. She circled the things that were non-negotiable, and after an hour she had a much more concise idea of where to start, but it occurred to her that she should head over to the big house and do one last walk-through before she finalized anything.

With the lists and contracts in hand, she hurried over before she lost the motivation. She moved as fast as she could, not just because she didn't want to find an excuse to put it off, but because she had to fight against the wind all the way there. Summer was definitely over, and it was looking like the cold and rainy autumn would be short as winter came in early.

Another reason to get the construction started soon, before it was held up by weather. Luckily the work she wanted done was indoors. At least most of it, but there were always slowdowns once the snow started. It could get deep and they didn't live all that close to town.

The road to the ranch was only plowed when Sam, or one of the workers, took a truck out to do it. There would be days when she and Sam would have to take care of the animals themselves, because the hands wouldn't be able to make it in at all, so she doubted she'd be able to count on contractors getting through.

But they'd work it out. Everything in her life was running along just fine for a change, so she could deal with a few delays if she had to.

She walked through the rooms making notes. Most of the highpoints she'd already pointed out when she discussed the renovations, but now she was looking at things with an eye towards planning. What could be done after they moved back in? Which things could be staggered so that the main space was livable?

It was easier to see what the most important changes were when she was right in the middle of it, and she finished making notes feeling a lot more positive about the direction she wanted to take. And then she stopped to take a minute. Change was hard sometimes. This was going to be painful, but it was also going to be good for her.

It was likely the last time she'd see the house looking untouched like this. Her childhood home with the faded wallpaper and half-painted walls that she'd been working on before she realized it needed more care than she could give. The plans were extensive and once they were complete it would be a whole different structure.

It went beyond cosmetic. She'd be breaking down walls to give the downstairs a more open layout and upstairs to make the bedrooms bigger. By the time everything was done, she hoped the last ghosts would be purged and she could settle into a home that was like new. A dream home that, best of all, would be right on the ranch she loved.

She was actually smiling when she headed for the back door, pretty sure she had everything she needed to make the calls and put things in motion. As she crossed the living room, she heard a knock. It didn't come from the back door, which meant it probably wasn't anyone who worked the ranch. They always went around to the kitchen.

It was a surprise, and good timing too since she was

rarely in the house anymore, but she wasn't expecting it to be anything important. Probably a salesman, or someone who had gotten turned around and lost, she figured. She opened the door to find an attractive, older woman standing on the porch and looking nervous.

She certainly didn't look like she was selling anything, with her tailored clothing and her carefully styled hair. Nothing about her said small town or local either. It was almost impossible to tell how old the woman was. She could have been anything from thirty-five to fifty, but there were fine lines on her face that weren't quite hidden by make-up and those said there should have been at least a little grey sprinkled into the black strands. It was probably dyed then, but not with cheap box dye. Nope, definitely expensive salon work there.

"Can I help you?" she asked, offering the woman a smile.

For a second the woman said nothing, and then her eyes went wide, and her mouth worked silently until she finally found her words. "Charlotte? Is—is that you?"

Charlie couldn't remember the last time someone had used her real name and she frowned. "Um, yeah. It's Charlie though. Do I know you?"

The woman let out an ear-piercing squeal that made Charlie wince. "Oh, my gawd! I can't believe it! Look at you —you're all grown up and beautiful!"

Charlie blinked and tilted her head as she examined the stranger. There was something vaguely familiar about her, but she couldn't place it. "Thanks. I've been grown up for a while now."

"I know, I know. And I should have come before, but—" She paused and laughed, waving a perfectly-manicured hand. "you know how time flies. Before you know it, years have gone by. I knew you were grown up, of course, I just—I didn't really believe it until now. Just look at you." She seemed to realize she was rattling on and came to an abrupt stop, shaking her head.

None of that had made much sense to Charlie and she was more confused than ever. There was that embarrassed feeling too, when someone obviously knew you, but you didn't remember them, and it left her feeling awkward. She couldn't think of a subtle way to get the information so finally she just asked the blunt question, "I'm sorry, do I know you?"

The woman seemed startled and then her face fell. In the sadness the lines deepened, causing Charlie to move the age approximation upwards. She was now guessing she had to be more like forty-five. Not that it helped her figure out who the woman was.

The stranger's eyes filled with tears and she sniffled. She looked down and began to root around in her designer purse, as she spoke. "I-I guess it was too much to expect you'd remember me. It's been a long time since you last saw me, I know. Of course, Jimmy sent me plenty of pictures when you were growing up, and I sent some back, but I guess he decided not to share them with you." She let out a long sigh, pulled a package of tissue out and began to dab at her eyes.

Somehow with all that talking she still hadn't managed to actually say who she was, and Charlie was starting to get antsy. She shifted, waiting to be enlightened, but not wanting to be rude about it. "I'm sorry," she said, because she wasn't sure what else to say.

Another dramatic sniffle. "No, Charlotte, *I'm* sorry. I should never have left you. A girl needs her mother, but at the time Jimmy was holding all the cards and it seemed like the best thing to do would be to leave." She stopped, laughed with a brittle sound and shook her head. "And I'm an idiot because you clearly have no idea what's going on and I keep babbling." She took a long deep breath. "My name is Vicky. Vicky Townsend now, but it used to be Vicky McGee."

Charlie stared at her blankly. Not because she wasn't understanding, but because she was flat out stunned and in shock.

But Vicky must have felt she needed to explain further. "I'm your mother, Charlotte."

"I—" Charlie stopped and closed her mouth. She knew she should be saying something, but she had no idea how she was supposed to respond. She didn't doubt it was true; once the words were out it was obvious. The familiar appearance, if you added twenty years to what she remembered, then yes it could be her.

"Sorry, I wasn't expecting … this is a shock," she said finally. She took a deep breath to steady herself, but her face felt numb. She couldn't make herself show the emotions she felt she should be expressing. A happy smile of welcome would be fake. Mother or not, she didn't know this woman.

"I understand, baby. I do. I wish I hadn't let things go on so long but there were reasons." Vicky paused, and a frown crossed her lips. "Your father insisted it would be better if I just cut ties, and he has a way of getting what he wants. He can be quite a bully at times, but the important thing is I'm here now." She dabbed under her eyes and tried to force a smile.

Charlie didn't know what she was feeling. Everything felt muffled and strained so the words about her father barely penetrated at first. When they did, she felt a pang of irritation. Her father had his faults, but he was gone now and talking him down seemed wrong. And then she realized with painful clarity.

She didn't know. Her mother didn't know that Jimmy was dead.

"Vicky..."

The older woman cut her off with a pleading, hopeful smile. "Oh please, don't. I know you haven't seen me in a long time, but it seems so strange to hear you call me that. Can't you call me mom?"

Charlie opened her mouth and then shut it with an audible snap. Mom? No, she definitely wasn't going to call her that. Instead of arguing she ignored it. "You know Jimmy died, right?"

Charlie winced at how blunt the words sounded coming out of her mouth. She hadn't meant them to be so cold, but shock had stolen away her ability to phrase things with more delicacy. The look on Vicky's face as she took in the words was odd. Charlie almost thought she saw irritation there for a second, but then dark eyes welled up with tears and she decided she had imagined it.

"What? Oh, no! I didn't ... I'm so sorry to ..." Her mother trailed off and she was back to dabbing at her eyes.

"Yeah, he had cancer. I guess no one knew where you were to let you know. It's been a while now." Charlie counted in her head and came up with just over four months since her father had died.

"Your father had my information, but I guess he didn't pass it on. I'm—wow, Jimmy. I really didn't expect ... he was so full of life, you know?" She was shaking her head and looked floored by the news, but Charlie didn't notice much grief.

Well, it had been a lot of years since they were married. Even before then they'd never seemed to get along very well, so it wasn't really a surprise, she supposed. She couldn't expect this stranger to feel the same level of hurt she did, just because once upon a time they'd been married and had a kid together.

Charlie hesitated and then stepped back and gestured inside. "Do you want to come in?"

Vicky nodded, offered her a slight smile, and preceded her through the door. She stopped just inside the door and looked around with a critical eye. "Not too much has changed on the old homestead, I see. Boy, this place brings back some memories." She turned, taking it all in, including the half-painted walls. "Trying to fix things up a little?"

"I was, but it turned out to be a lot more work than I expected, so we're hiring people to come in and give it a whole new look. Actually, you're lucky you caught me here. I was just making some last-minute notes on what I wanted done," Charlie explained.

Her hand went up in a nervous gesture, tucking her hair back behind her ears. She hadn't bothered with her usual ponytail and she was very aware of how messy she was, especially next to her mother who would probably never be seen in public looking less than perfect.

Vicky stopped and turned to her. "Oh? You're not staying here then?"

"Um, not right now, no. I'm living over in the foreman's cabin … with Sam." She wasn't sure why she felt embarrassed to admit she was living with a man. It wasn't like her mother had any parental authority over her, nevertheless she could feel a slight heat rising in her face. "He's the foreman," she added.

"I'm aware. Your father mentioned him a few times." Vicky's tone and expression were hard to read. She seemed to be going for neutral but under that, Charlie sensed something else … disappointment maybe?

"We're seeing each other. He's a really great guy. I think you'll like him." Charlie stopped short. Why was she explaining that to her mother or acting like the woman would even be staying around to meet him?

She changed the subject, "Anyway, it made more sense to live over there. Less chaos once the renovations start."

"Are you starting soon?" There was more than casual curiosity there.

Charlie glanced at her and then looked away. "Um, not sure. I have to accept one of the bids first and then schedule things. It might take a while to actually get things going, but I'm hoping to make progress before winter slows things down."

"Hmm." Vicky began to move around the room, touching things and picking them up with a restless energy.

Charlie wondered if she was looking for memories. If so, she probably wouldn't find much. Jimmy hadn't been the sentimental type and he'd gotten rid of most of the knick-knacks years ago. "Is ... something wrong?"

Her mother stopped and let out a long sigh. "The truth is, Charlie, I was hoping your father would let me stay here for a few days. And now, well ..."

"Stay here? With Dad? Uh, why would—" She cut herself off abruptly because her first reaction was not a very nice one. She couldn't imagine why her father would have wanted the ex-wife who left him to come and stay in his house.

"I don't want to speak badly of your father, Charlie, but he *clearly* left you out of the loop on a number of things. The reality is, we've stayed in contact all these years and if I'm being honest, he owed me for giving in to his wishes with you."

She held up a hand, even though Charlie hadn't made the slightest motion to interrupt. "I know, Jimmy was always your favorite. From the moment you could walk it was always him you ran to, but he wasn't a perfect man, Charlie. I'm sure you've gotten a few ideas about me from the way I left, but things were more complicated than you know."

Charlie's eyes narrowed and she stayed silent as she tried to work through that. Since learning that her father had kept a few secrets from her, she had to accept that it was possible that there were more. Her mind flashed to the letter he'd left her. The one she'd yet to read. Maybe it had some of the answers she was looking for.

"So, you think Dad was going to let you stay here? I really don't—that doesn't sound much like Jimmy."

"He *owed* me. He made certain promises that, well, he didn't keep. I'm in a rough spot right now, partly because of him, so yes, I was hoping to stay here while I sorted things out. I didn't realize ... no one told me that ..." She trailed off with another long sigh and then she took a seat on the couch as though all the energy had gone out of her.

Charlie felt awkward standing there alone, so she moved over and sat in the chair across from her mother. "What do you mean he owed you for giving into his wishes? What wishes?"

Vikki sniffled. Her eyes were wet with tears, but as always, the tissue was there to catch them before they could ruin her eyeliner. "Oh, Charlie, you didn't really think I wanted to leave you *here*, did you? A ranch is no place for a little girl. I wanted to take you off to the city where you would have every advantage, but your father ..." She waved a hand sharply.

Charlie stared, stunned. It was the biggest shock in a day that had been filled with them, and she could feel her heart starting to thump hard in her chest. Suddenly she wished Sam was there. She always felt better when he was there and the last thing she wanted to do was breakdown in front of this stranger.

Her mother had wanted her? Had wanted to take her? Jimmy had never said, never even hinted, that Vicky would have brought Charlie with her. He certainly had never mentioned that he was the one to insist Charlie stay.

She felt sick. Her head was spinning, and her mouth was filled with cotton. How could he have kept this from her, and more importantly why? She loved the ranch, always had since she was too young to even walk, so moving to the city would have sucked. Part of her was glad if Jimmy did put his foot down on that.

But he'd never told her or given her the slightest hint that her mother hadn't just strolled out the door into a new life, and never looked back. It would have meant so much to the lost little girl she'd been to know that her mother had regretted leaving her and had wanted to take her too.

Maybe she wouldn't be such a mess of anxiety and relationship issues if she'd known ... her hands were starting to shake, and she forced those thoughts down. Just because her mother said something didn't mean it was actually true and she needed to remember that.

Believing it would have been easier if Jimmy's death hadn't already left her feeling confused and betrayed.

CHAPTER 6

Sam walked through the door whistling as he dropped his keys on the counter with the usual clatter. He'd been in a good mood all day, the night before had kept a smile on his face, and he noticed some of the hands giving him the side-eye as they wondered what was going on. But the truth was his mood had improved drastically ever since things with Charlie had started to go right.

It all felt right. Too good to be true really, but it seemed like they'd worked through the hardest parts and he was looking forward to smooth sailing. Which was why, when he came in to find silence and a dark house he was confused, but not really worried. Charlie hadn't worked that day. The labor was tapering off as they headed into winter and she wasn't needed most days.

She could have been out running errands, but one of the rules they'd put into place was that she was supposed to tell him when she went off the property. Not that he was being overprotective, but a lot of things could happen on the back roads, especially once the weather started getting bad. He wanted to know if she was out just in case.

And besides that, she'd been making an effort to have dinner waiting, or at least a plan for their meal when he came in from working a long day; something he'd come to appreciate highly. It had been her idea, an activity to keep her busy since she wasn't working much, but he had to admit it made his life a lot easier.

The kitchen was dark and there was no sign of food, but he'd been wrong. Charlie *was* there, sitting on the couch with the lights off. A small sniffle caught his attention and when he turned on the lamp there she was.

"You okay, baby?" He moved to her side quickly, concerned.

She was tucked in a corner with her legs pulled up to her chest. He couldn't see her face, with her hair spilling forward to cover it—for a second, he had a flashback to the night before as he reached out to push it back behind her ear. But the look on her face at the moment was far from happy. Her eyes were red and swollen and it was clear she'd been crying for a while.

He sat down next to her and scooped her into his lap. "Hey, what happened, darlin'?" He thought maybe something had reminded her of her father and set her off. That happened sometimes. She was still processing the grief and the pain would sneak up on her.

She shook her head and buried her face against his chest. As she clung to him a fresh spate of tears erupted, and he was left feeling helpless. He rubbed her back in slow gentle circles and whispered soothing things to her, but until she told him what was going on there was nothing else he could do.

The words came slowly, in short bursts, and they were hard to understand. At first, he couldn't figure out what she was trying to say. But when it all clicked, he understood why she was so upset. Anyone would be shocked to have a long-lost parent suddenly show up out of the blue. And the revelation that maybe she hadn't been lost by her own choice, but by Jimmy's—well, that had to be painful.

Charlie was taking his death hard and struggling with guilt over her (in his opinion) reasonable anger at him. This wasn't going to make any of it easier. "Damn. I—I'm sorry, Charlie girl. That's a whole hell of a lot to take in." He sighed and settled back, shifting her in his arms until she was lying against him in a more comfortable position.

"So, is she staying in town? Or did she just go back to wherever she came from?" He smoothed her hair.

Charlie stiffened in his arms, going tense. She mumbled something he couldn't hear, and he had to ask her to repeat it.

"I t-told her she could stay in the house for a while," she admitted in a small voice.

"You ... what? Charlie, are you sure that's a good idea?" He did his best not to sound like he was mad or judging her for the decision. If it had been his to make, he wasn't sure what he would have done either.

"No, no I'm not but I didn't know what else to do. She's in a bad place and she was expecting my father to help. I don't —I don't know if he would have helped her, but she seemed to think he owed her, and you know how Jimmy was about his debts and promises."

Her father was an honorable sort who did his best to keep his word and always paid off his debts, so yes, if he owed Charlie's mother, he might have put her up for a while. But the truth was, and he didn't want to point this out to Charlie, they didn't know if she was telling them the whole story.

"I don't know, Charlie girl. It all sounds kind of ..." He trailed off, and then sighed. It was one of those times when being her Daddy and bossing her around conflicted with decisions she needed to make for herself. He would have sent the woman packing because he had a bad feeling about the whole thing.

But it was her house and her mother. It was a complicated mess and as much as he wanted to step in and take the burden from her, he knew he couldn't—not unless she asked him to.

"I know, Sam. I do know. It's just ... aside from that it's my chance to maybe get to know her. Is that wrong? I know I shouldn't get invested in this, but I've always wondered what it would have been like if she stayed. And I just ..." The words were cut off, replaced with muffled sobbing as she pressed her face against his work shirt.

He had a sense of foreboding. He'd known Jimmy as well as anyone and his instincts told him that if Jimmy had kept her mom out of the picture there was a reason. Still, it wasn't what Charlie wanted to hear just then. All he could do was comfort her as she cried and listen as she vented her feelings.

Eventually she wore herself out. She didn't seem sleepy so instead of tucking her in he tried something else. "Why don't you let me take care of you tonight, Charlie. Just relax and let me handle things, okay?"

She sniffled and nodded. He released her, tucking her back into the corner of the couch and covering her with a blanket.

"I'm going to make some hot cocoa," he explained as he got up. Her face brightened immediately, and he ruffled her hair before heading to the kitchen. He could see her easily from where he was and could be by her side in a second if she started to cry again.

Charlie's inner child only peeked out on rare occasions, mostly when she was upset, but he cherished those moments because it meant he got to take care of her. He'd come to realize that their relationship went beyond Daddy kink for him. He was very much a Daddy Dom and while Charlie wasn't a Little, she did sometimes need that kind of affectionate parental care.

They didn't really try to define it any deeper than that and there was no reason to. When she was sad or scared, she slipped into a more vulnerable mindset. It felt younger to him, though not in an ageplay way. It was more that she needed him deeply, needed him to take over and he was happy to do so.

When he brought the hot cocoa back to her, she reached for the steaming mug eagerly. "Be careful, Charlie girl. Don't burn yourself," he warned her.

She rolled her eyes at that, but when his eyebrow went up, she immediately settled down and remembered her manners. "Thank you, Daddy. This is exactly what I needed."

She blew on it gently, but he knew her patience would give out before it was cool, and she'd end up burning her mouth on it. She always did and he always shook his head with a complete lack of surprise.

And just as he completed that thought she gave up blowing and took a hasty sip. It played out exactly as expected and he couldn't help laughing. "Every time, Charlie. Every single time."

"I can't help it. It smells too good to wait."

"Uh-huh." He turned to the cold fireplace and went to work building a fire. Nothing relaxed Charlie more than a fire; he felt the same. It took him a few minutes to get the kindling going before he could add in some larger pieces of wood, but once it was crackling cheerfully, he settled back on the couch and pulled her into his lap again.

She nestled against his chest, tucking her head under his chin as his arms wrapped around her. Their sex life was fantastic, the kinky parts were always exciting and never ceased to be interesting, but this... these quiet moments where they could just be together meant everything to him.

He loved her with all his heart and their relationship was growing into more than he could ever have hoped for. He just hoped her mother showing up wasn't going to cause a problem.

Almost as if she knew where his thoughts had gone, she sighed. "You think it was a mistake to let her stay, don't you?"

He rubbed her back in small gentle circles and thought about how to answer the question without upsetting her. "I think that Jimmy usually had reasons for the things he did, but I can't always say I agree with them. Without knowing the whole story ... I just can't say, Charlie."

She didn't speak for a while, and he was starting to think she'd fallen asleep in his lap when she finally spoke up again. "I think maybe it will be good for me. One way or the other it could clear up some of my baggage."

"Maybe, but Charlie, you do need to be careful. I don't want you getting hurt and you really don't know this woman, even if she's your mom—wait... are you actually sure she's your mom? I mean, did she show you proof?"

It suddenly occurred to him that Charlie was now fairly well-off. She wasn't going to be buying mansions, but she had a decent chunk of change tied up in stocks and investments. That kind of money tended to lure in predators like a wounded cow attracted coyotes.

She shifted, leaning back to look up at him with a frown on her face. "No ... I guess I didn't think to ask. I mean it would have been rude, but I suppose I need to make sure." She rolled her bottom lip under and bit it as she thought about it. "Oh, Mike would know. I mean he's been here forever. He must have met her back then."

Sam nodded, "Might be a good idea to bring him over to the house tomorrow for a 'reunion' just to be sure and then we can go from there."

Just having a next step in place seemed to make Charlie

feel better and she relaxed back against him while they watched the fire. Sam wasn't feeling nearly as relaxed and his thoughts were turbulent as he considered the many ways that this could end up hurting his girl.

She did finally fall asleep in his arms and he picked her up carefully and carried her into the bedroom. She barely roused as he undressed her and tucked her under the covers. He slipped her stuffed bunny into her arms in case her dreams turned dark, and then he went to make himself dinner.

His stomach growled angrily, not surprising since he'd gotten used to eating as soon as he walked in the door. He dug around in the fridge and threw together a few sandwiches as a quick meal. He ate them in front of the fire, so lost in thought he barely noticed them disappearing bite by bite until the plate was empty.

If Charlie's mother was there to get to know her daughter, then he was all for them reconnecting. If she just needed a place to stay for a few weeks he was fine with that too. The big house had plenty of space and it would probably take at least that long for construction work to start.

But if this woman, who had appeared out of nowhere, was there to cause Charlie pain then he was going to have to find a way to deal with the situation. She would want to handle this on her own; she was stubborn that way. He had no choice but to let her, but that wasn't going to stop him from doing some snooping in the meantime just to make sure things were legit.

She'd had a good idea about talking to Mike, and he planned to have a conversation with him as well. If that didn't pan out, he could always hit up the lawyer who managed the estate. With the way the trust was set up, Sam had no choice but to confer with the lawyer on a monthly basis about the budget and over time he'd come to respect Morris.

He went to bed planning to take care of both of those things first thing in the morning, but things didn't end up going that way. Instead, they woke up to a whole passel of new problems, not unusual ones for a ranch, but it kept him busy the whole morning.

The weather had taken a turn and the blustery autumn winds had switched to rain, which at some point early in the morning had frozen over into a solid sheet of ice. He discovered this when he set foot outside the door and promptly landed on his ass with a bellow of pain that had Charlie running to see what happened.

"Sam! Are you okay?" She leaned out, to get a better look but seemed hesitant to try to get to him in case she ended up landing in the same situation. "The weatherman needs a new job. He didn't say anything about freezing temperatures yesterday."

But they both knew that the reports could be wildly unpredictable in their area. The mountains created their own little weather system. "I'm alright. Just my pride, I think. I landed on my ass."

"Usually when someone gets a sore butt it means they were naughty. Were you a bad Daddy?" Charlie asked, with innocence dripping from every word.

He growled. "Girl, you're lucky I can't get to you right now or I'd show you a sore butt. Go get the salt for the stairs." There was a big bag of it just inside the door and he was glad he'd thought to stock up early.

As she started sprinkling the steps liberally, he made a second attempt to get up. He gave her credit for not laughing outright as she watched him do a wild flailing dance before he crashed back down again. After the second fall he just lay there on his back, staring up at the foreboding grey sky and let out a long sigh. "It's way too early for this shit," he grumbled.

But the salt started to work, just not as fast as he would have liked. He was freezing and, in the end, he still had to half-crawl back into the house to avoid another slip. He ignored the expression on Charlie's face as she made every effort not to laugh at how comical he'd looked.

"Okay, I'm officially starting this morning over. I'm getting back in the shower, and I'm going to pretend like this never happened," he said. He needed another hot shower too, mostly because he was chilled to the bone and his clothes were soaked anyway.

He took a minute to grab his phone and call Ben to warn him about the ice. Chances were good he'd already noticed, but sometimes they got hit with very localized weather effects, so it was better to let him know. His second had gate keys and was usually the first in, so he could go out and sand the dirt road if it needed it.

By the time he was out of his second shower of the day, dressed, and ready to make another attempt he was running nearly an hour later than usual. But the salt had pitted the ice until it was safer, and Charlie had filled a thermos with hot coffee for him to take.

"I take it the horses are staying in today?" she asked.

Normally the horses were out all day but stabled at night. They tried to keep them in the stalls as little as possible because they didn't get much exercise in there but once the weather changed the balance shifted.

"Yeah, not risking a leg while it's this slippery. Maybe in the afternoon if the ice melts. I guess we'll have to move the cows over to the winter fields sooner than planned too." He was resigned but not happy about the speeding timetable. It had been almost a sure bet that they had a few more weeks to prepare, but he'd manage.

He dug his ice grips out of the closet and wrapped them around the bottom of his work boots. There wouldn't be any slipping with those in place.

"Do you think you can get by without me today? I know I was supposed to work, but ..."

He knew exactly what the but was. She wanted to go see her mother, and since he wanted to have a talk with Mike privately that worked out for him. "I think we can get by," he said.

"Thanks, Sam! If you need me just send someone to the big house to let me know." She threw her arms around his shoulders in a grateful hug and he turned to drop a light kiss on her cheek.

"Just remember what I said and be careful until we know what's going on, okay?"

"I will. I promise," she assured him.

Now why didn't he believe that? Well, maybe it wouldn't be a problem, only time would tell. For now, he grabbed the thermos and headed to the main barn. It was a lot easier with the grips on, but the first thing he was going to need to do was spread some sand around or it wouldn't just be animals he had to worry about breaking things.

By the time the ranch hands started to arrive, with Ben in the lead of course, he'd cleared a path to the barn. Everyone scuttled inside to get warm as he passed out assignments for the morning. He was hoping that by the time afternoon rolled around the sun would be out.

Once the ice was melted, he'd be sending most of them off to move the cattle herd into the winter pastures where they could be fed and watered more easily. He wasn't taking the ice as a fluke event, but assuming it was a sign of an early winter and he had to plan accordingly.

It meant rearranging his plans but that was the way things went when your job was ruled by the weather. As everyone headed off to work, he motioned for Mike to join him in his office, and he closed the door so they wouldn't be overheard.

"Somethin' up, Sam?" Mike didn't look concerned, not the way some of the younger guys would have been. He knew his job and did it well. The chances of Sam calling him in to bitch at him were exactly zero.

"Maybe..." Sam parked his butt on the corner of the desk and sighed. "We've got an unexpected guest up at the house." He stopped there, trying to figure out how to phrase it. "Seems like Charlie's mom is in town."

Mike's bushy white eyebrows went up in surprise. "Vicky? Vicky's here?"

"Yeah, well, at least that's what she says. Charlie hasn't seen her since she was in the single digits so I did wonder how we could even be sure it was her."

"So, you were thinking maybe I could verify?" Mike asked. He shrugged. "I haven't seen her since then either but I'm pretty sure I'll recognize her if you want me to wander over there at some point today." His tone was neutral; it seemed to Sam that it was kept that way deliberately.

"I'd appreciate that, but I'd also like to pick your brain about ... Well, it seems like she's telling Charlie that Jimmy kept her away deliberately and I don't know if that's true, but it's got her upset. You know she's not thrilled with the ranch situation but she's just starting to settle down and I really don't want her riled up."

Mike frowned hard, the lines in his forehead deepened into canyons. "The thing is, Sam, I wouldn't be surprised if that was true. Jimmy and Vicky were always fighting over the ranch, over damn near everything, but especially over Charlie." He reached up and rubbed the back of his neck.

"So, you think Jimmy would have kept her from seeing Charlie because they didn't get along?" Sam was skeptical.

Vicky's absence had hurt Charlie and her father wouldn't have wanted that.

"No. Look, Sam, I'm not really one to tell tales but Vicky isn't someone I'd want raising a kid. Her priorities are Vicky first, Vicky last, and maybe if there's anything left, she might consider someone else. We never got along, in fact she pushed Jimmy to fire me. And I'm not going to get into why I think she'd do that, but I'm saying ... if Jimmy kept her out of the picture then he had good reason."

Mike wasn't a big talker, for him that was pretty much a whole speech, and after that Sam couldn't get anything else out of him. He'd said what he wanted to say and that was that. With the excuse that he had work to do, Mike vanished out the door before Sam could interrogate him any further.

The talk clinched his gut feeling that this was going to go badly. Later that day he found a scrawled note from Mike on his desk. It stated simply: *It's her.* He rubbed his temples as a tension headache started to grow.

He would tell Charlie what Mike said. She respected Mike's opinion, thought of him as family. She'd listen and ask Vicky to leave and they'd get on with their lives. Only that turned out to be wishful thinking on his part.

When he walked in the door just after sundown, he found the house brightly lit, the fire crackling merrily, and Charlie singing in the kitchen as she cooked dinner. He stopped just inside the door to watch her. She was wearing earbuds and didn't hear him, so he had a moment to enjoy the expression of contentment and happiness on her face as she danced around the small area.

When she turned around and saw him there, she jumped. Her mouth opened in a comical 'O' of surprise. "You scared me!" It was almost a shout and he motioned to her ears.

"You look happy tonight. Good news?" he asked when she removed them. Inside he was hoping she'd tell him she was excited because she'd picked a contractor, or had applied for the doctoral program, or anything that didn't involve her mother.

"Nope. I just had a nice day. Vicky and I talked all morning and then we had lunch together and baked cookies. It was really nice." She waved a hand at a plate of chocolate chip cookies on the table and he picked one up.

Instead of eating it he examined it, turning it over in his hands like he expected to find the secrets of the universe scrawled on the bottom. She didn't seem to notice his quiet and continued on, telling him about her day as she stirred the pot on the stove.

"I always wondered what it would be like to have a mom around. I guess this is it. I'm really mad I missed out on all of those years, but we're going to make up for it. She said—"

"Charlie."

"—that we could go shopping together and I know that sounds silly, but I remember when I was a teenager, I always wished she was around to help me pick out clothes. I –"

"Charlotte." He used her full name to make sure he had her attention as he walked over and pulled her around to look at him.

She blinked. "What's wrong?"

"Remember what we talked about last night? About not getting too invested in this until we found out some facts?"

Her bottom lip trembled, just for a second, and he almost thought he had imagined it. There was no sign of the upset a second later as she laughed. "Oh, yeah, don't worry about it. I got her to show me her driver's license. I mean, it was awkward, and I didn't want her to know I doubted that she was my mom, so I had to come up with a reason to—"

He gave her a gentle shake to cut her off. He'd never seen her like this, so bubbly and excited. It was as though she thought if she talked fast enough it would make all the doubts disappear. "Charlie, I know you're excited about this, but I need you to calm down and listen to me."

"Why? What's wrong, Sam?" Her mouth was already forming a pout and this time he knew he didn't imagine the lip wobble.

"I talked to Mike, and yeah he confirmed it's your mom so that part is all true, but we still don't know if the rest of her story is fact. Jimmy isn't here to ask and Mike... Mike doesn't seem real fond of her."

"Why, what did he say?"

"He said she tried to get him fired. That maybe if Jimmy kept her away from you it was for a good reason." He watched the expressions rushing across her face and could see how conflicted she was. What she wanted to be true compared with what she knew... it was tough, and he couldn't make it any easier.

"I'm sure there's a good reason for all of that. Sometimes people just don't get along. It doesn't mean either one is a bad person." But she sounded uncertain and the excitement in her voice had dimmed audibly.

"Yeah, I get that, Charlie. But I feel like you're throwing your whole heart into this relationship with her and I'm afraid you're going to get hurt."

"I just want it to be real, Daddy." She threw her arms around him and buried herself against his work shirt, clinging hard enough to knock the air out of his lungs. He could feel the fabric getting damp and knew she was crying again.

He began to rub her back with one hand. He reached around and slid the pot off the heat so it wouldn't burn and then scooped her up and carried her to the bedroom. He settled them both on the bed so he could hold her in his arms as she cried.

It seemed like she'd been doing a lot of that lately, and

maybe it was good for her. She sometimes had trouble letting out all the grief and emotions she struggled with, unless she was spanked to tears. Crying without needing that physical push might be healthy for her, but it did leave him feeling helpless.

He understood tears after getting spanked and knew exactly what to do and how to handle it. Tears from emotional trauma were a little more difficult and he wanted to tell her everything would be fine and of course her mom loved her, because that's what she wanted so badly to hear.

The problem was he didn't believe it. Maybe he was wrong, but he felt like there was more going on then what Vicky was telling her. Reassuring Charlie now would probably end up with his girl being crushed later if her mother did turn out to have an agenda.

Being the Dom in the relationship was hard sometimes and the answers didn't just drop out of the sky no matter how much he wished they would. He pulled her back against his chest, spooning her. He wanted her to feel his strength at her back and know he was there to protect her as much as he could.

The problem was he didn't think this was something he could protect her from, not really. "You know I want you to be happy, baby," he whispered against her ear. "I really hope she's here to finally be the mom you missed out on growing up."

She sniffled. "But you don't believe it, do you?"

He took a deep breath and then let it out in a long sigh. "No, I don't, but I'm willing to give her the benefit of the doubt for now. I just really need for you to not get swept away in the reunion until you're sure she's not here for another reason. I'm not going to let anyone hurt you, not even you, babygirl."

She was quiet for a minute and as the silence stretched

out, he wondered if she was going to argue it. "I guess … this is kind of what I asked for, right? When I asked you to be my Dom?"

"Kind of yeah. I admit I never expected this exact problem but keeping you from being self-destructive is way up on my list of important things, Charlie."

She wiggled out of his arms and sat up on the edge of the bed. He leaned up on one elbow and waited to see what she was going to do. He half-expected a tantrum of some sort, but she surprised him.

"You're right. I don't know her. I don't know her motives or why she's here. Even though Jimmy kept some secrets from me, I can't believe he'd keep my mom away just to be cruel to her, especially not when it was hurting me too. I know my dad loved me, despite the mess with the will."

There was a tinge of bitterness there and he knew she still hadn't resolved her feelings about that issue. "I agree. Jimmy wasn't a cruel or vindictive man and even though I didn't always agree with his choices for you … I always knew he was making them because he thought they were best."

"Yeah." She got up and began to pace the floor. Her forehead was furrowed with concentration. He just watched in silence and let her work through her thoughts. Eventually she worked off some of the nervous energy and came to a stop in front of him.

He could see she was working up to say something significant, but he had no clue what it would be. Sometimes his Charlie was unpredictable. He waited silently to find out what was on her mind.

CHAPTER 7

It took her a few seconds to decide what she wanted to say, because all of this was weighing on her emotionally and she was afraid of making the wrong choices. "Okay, so I know I agreed with you that I couldn't really trust her, and I know I said I'd try not to get too …"

"Invested?" he suggested.

That was exactly the right word. "Yeah, that. But that was before I spent the day with her, and whether she's trying to manipulate me or not the whole mom thing is really sucking me in. She could probably be the worst person in the world and I'd still want to give it a shot, but the fact that she seems really regretful and sad about missing me grow up just makes it so much harder to maintain my distance."

She looked at him, waiting for his response, waiting for him to tell her what to do about it because she really had no idea. He was the Dom, he had to have the answers, right?

"Are you asking me to step in?" He sounded wary and she didn't blame him.

"Yes. No. Fuck, I don't know, maybe?" She laughed at how ridiculous she sounded. "Just keep my feet on the ground, okay? Keep reminding me that I don't really know her. Remind me that I've made it this long without her, so if she bails, I'll be fine."

There was a skeptical expression on his face as if he were already picturing how much work that was going to be and she couldn't even say he was wrong. After only one day with her mother, she felt—she felt like she wanted more. It was like every single thing she'd never gotten to do with her mom was crowding in to get on the activity list.

She had no idea how long Vicky was going to stay and she wanted to take advantage of every minute while she had the chance. So, while she agreed with everything Sam was saying, she just didn't know if she'd be able to resist when her own heart was telling her to go for it.

"I can do that, Charlie, but I'm going to remind you that you asked for this when you get mad at me."

When not if; he knew her so well. She couldn't deny that either. "That's fair."

"Good, now let's go eat. I'm starving and you're not missing dinner two nights in a row," Sam said as he got off the bed. His stomach made a lout growling sound to punctuate his words.

She rolled her eyes as she followed him to the kitchen to start dinner cooking again, but the truth was she loved his protective side. Those little touches and moments when he took care of her meant a lot. The submissive side of her enjoyed doing things for him in return and that was one reason she'd started cooking his dinner most nights when she wasn't working with him.

There was something grounding in a daily task that obviously pleased him so much. Watching his face light up when he came through the door tired and saw that dinner was cooking pleased her on a very basic level. Sitting across from each other to eat was special too.

She was discovering that so many of the things that seemed boring or silly from the outside really did a lot to build up a relationship. In some ways it felt like this was her first adult romance. When they'd dated before she'd still lived under her father's roof and there was a certain amount of sneaking around even after they were both over eighteen.

Now they were living together, and it all felt different, but in a good way. Sitting there and talking about their day like an old married couple—she cut the thought off there and waited for the wave of panic that usually followed any thought of marriage. Seconds went by but nothing happened.

She slowly relaxed and finally smiled as she settled back in her chair. Getting to know Vicky was helping, she was sure of it. Of course, she knew what Sam would say. Or at least, she played out what she thought he'd say in her head.

Just because you thought of us married and didn't have a panic attack once doesn't mean anything Charlie. You don't have one every time, do you?

And he'd be right, she didn't get anxious every single time she thought about their relationship deepening, but still she was choosing to take it as a good sign. She ignored the niggling thought in the back of her head warning her to be careful.

Despite all the earlier tears she was back to being in a good mood and enjoyed the conversation with Sam. But it was natural that eventually the conversation would roll around to the things she was supposed to be getting done.

"Did you decide on the contractor yet?"

She nodded and waited until her mouth wasn't full so she could explain her new plans. "I did, and I did put in a call to tell them I was accepting their estimate, but I told them we wanted to wait a few weeks before we got started on the actual work. They'll be coming around to get measurements and make supply lists though."

His eyebrow went up. "Why the delay? With this early winter coming on that might not be the best idea."

She shifted in her chair and kept her eyes focused on the plate in front of her. "Well Vicky said a couple weeks would be enough to get her back on her feet, so I figured it would be easier for her if they weren't tearing everything up over there."

After the conversation they'd just had she was expecting another lecture, but Sam just sighed. "Figured it was that. Well, I guess two weeks won't hurt much."

"It might be a little longer than that if—"

He gave her a look and shook his head. "Two weeks and the construction starts. If she needs to stay longer then she'll just have to put up with the mess, right?"

"But..."

"Right, Charlie?" His voice went hard and so did his expression.

She sighed. "Yes Daddy. I'll tell them we want it to start in two weeks. I guess we can have them do it one floor at a time if she's still here." They'd already discussed doing it that way so it wouldn't be that big of a deal, hopefully.

Her mother *had* arrived unexpectedly after all and couldn't just expect them to change everything for her without warning anyway, could she? But there had been some strong hinting that Charlie *should* put it off so Vicky could stay there and that was what made Charlie decide to postpone it. She'd been so eager and rushed to get things started and then somehow when Vicky subtly brought up how nice it would be if things could be delayed... it had felt reasonable to do that.

But apparently Sam didn't feel the same way. He was probably right.

"Good." He seemed like he wanted to say something else

but then he just shook his head and went back to concentrating on his meal.

She had a feeling it would have been another warning about Vicky, but he probably figured he'd already made his point. And he had, but it was a point that was going to keep coming up over the next few weeks because it never seemed to stick when she was out of his sight.

She tried to take what he'd said into account whenever she spent time with her mother, but before she knew it, she'd be laughing and having a good time and she'd forget. The woman was starting to feel less like a stranger and more like a real mom every day. They did things together, mostly shopping and lunches out since Vicky had absolutely zero interest in the ranch. She didn't even want to look around to see how things had changed in all the years she'd been gone.

"No thanks, I had enough of mud and flies when I lived here. More than enough to last a lifetime," she said with a delicate sniff that seemed full of derision.

Charlie shouldn't have been surprised at that since from what she'd heard the ranch was a big part of the problem between her parents. It just seemed weird to her that anyone could hate such a beautiful place. And even people who didn't care for the ranch or the cows usually moved past it to enjoy looking at the horses, but Vicky was adamant that she didn't want to get any closer than the house itself.

Charlie didn't want to argue so she gave in and invariably they ended up doing whatever Vicky wanted to do. After the first few days she started to notice that her mother looked worried any time she paid for things. A pinched anxious look would cross the older woman's face and for a moment she'd actually looked her age.

Charlie realized that money was probably the basis for Vicky needing a place to stay so she took over and paid the bills when they went out. She didn't mind. She had plenty of money and it's not like the costs were high for a few shopping trips or restaurants.

Vicky even talked her into taking a trip to the big city for a girls' day out and they spent the night in a fancy hotel. It had been a lot of fun and they'd both had quite a bit more to drink than they should have in the hotel bar, which left them giggling and hanging onto each other all the way to their room. They stayed up late and told each other stories about their lives.

It was exactly the kind of deep conversation she'd always wanted to have with her mom. On the long drive home the next afternoon Charlie felt completely happy. The short trip had been a real bonding experience, she thought. It was around then that she gave in and started calling her mom instead of Vicky.

She did feel a small pang of nervousness about it. It felt like she was taking down one of her walls and there was a sense of making herself vulnerable. But after getting to know each other so well it seemed rude to continue to call her by her first name.

That trip was a turning point in her relationship with her mother and though Sam continued to look concerned and warn her to be careful, it was obvious he knew it was a losing battle and seemed to take it in stride. He didn't complain that she was rarely home to make dinner anymore or remind her that doing it had been her idea to start with.

He accepted that she was wrapped up with getting to know her mother finally and didn't grumble (much) that suddenly he seemed to get very little time with her as a result. But he put his foot down when she started shirking her duties.

She didn't realize she was in trouble until he stomped up the wooden back stairs of the big house, stormed into the kitchen and glared at her with flinty eyes. "Forget something, Charlie?"

She set down her cup of coffee and frowned as her stomach did the sinking thing. She recognized the expression on his face and knew she'd messed up, but she had no idea what she'd done. "Um... maybe? Why?"

"We were shorthanded today and you were supposed to help with the herds, remember?" One eyebrow went up so high it disappeared under his messy hair.

Damn. She did remember now that he'd mentioned it. She'd just completely lost track. "Whoops. I'm sorry! I can come now."

"Darlin' it's after five, we're done. I didn't have time to come over and grab you when we needed you. This is the second time this week and I warned you before, so you know what that means."

Her stomach did a slow queasy roll and she winced. She knew exactly what that meant, and she wasn't looking forward to it. She dropped her gaze to the scarred old table and nodded.

"I'll see you in the barn in fifteen minutes then."

"Um—is something wrong?"

They both turned to look at Vicky standing in the kitchen doorway. Her mother was frowning as her gaze shifted from Charlie to Sam and back again.

Charlie had somehow forgotten that her mother was there and had just gone to use the bathroom. She was lucky that Sam hadn't been more explicit with the threat because that was a conversation she wasn't ready to have with her mother—now or ever.

As it was, she didn't think Vicky could possibly guess what any of it meant which was a huge relief. "No, mom, everything is fine. I just forgot I was supposed to go out to the winter pasture to help today so I'm going to go help Sam out in a few minutes instead."

"But we were just going to make dinner … are you sure you have to go? I really hate eating alone," she said in a sad little voice. She shot a pleading look at Sam. "I'm sure he doesn't need your help, right?"

Charlie shifted in her chair. "Well, I—" That was how Vicky usually got her to stay later than she'd planned. She sounded so sad to see Charlie go and it made her feel awful so she would put off leaving.

Sam wasn't swayed by the sad voice and pitiful looks. "Actually ma'am, I *do* need her in the barn. I'm sure she'll have some time to visit with you tomorrow, but for now she's got chores to take care of," he said firmly.

Charlie started to get up obediently; she really didn't want to get herself in any more trouble. "I'll see you tomorrow, Mom."

The sadness dropped away like a mask and Vicky's expression turned bitter. "This is ridiculous. A big strong man like you can't possibly need a lady's help. And Charlie, you're the owner. You don't need to let him boss you around, just because you're sleeping together."

Charlie swallowed hard and she sent a pleading look in Sam's direction, mutely begging him not to start a fight with her mother. "Mom, that's not how it works around here. And I'm only half-owner. Sam owns the other half and he's the one in charge, legally."

Her mother looked just as thunderstruck as she'd felt that day in the lawyer's office. "What? Jimmy left half to *him*? He's just a worker!" Appalled didn't even begin to describe her tone.

Charlie winced and looked at Sam. "I'll talk to her."

He narrowed his eyes, glared at Vicky and jerked his head

sharply. "I'll see you in the barn. Fifteen minutes, don't be late."

She waited for him to go and then turned back to her mother. "Mom, Sam has been the foreman here since he was a teenager. His father was the foreman before that. Jimmy trusted him to run things and ... I admit I was upset to find out he'd left things this way, but Sam's really good at his job, so it's probably for the best."

Vicky didn't seem to be taking in what Charlie had said. Instead, she'd begun to pace back and forth muttering. "I can't believe your father. It's one thing to treat me like trash all these years, but I thought he'd at least make sure you were taken care of. I can't believe he gave your inheritance away to some random ranch hand."

"Mom, Sam isn't just some random hand. He's the best person to run things and dad made sure I was taken care of. Sam just got half the ranch—the house here is mine, and all the stocks and investments. I have more than enough," she explained. It struck her as funny to be arguing the other side of this.

She was still mad at her father, but she wasn't going to let Vicky think badly about him. She kept the specific details of the will to herself, but what she'd disclosed was enough to get her mother's attention.

"Stocks? Investments? What are you talking about?"

"Yeah, it was a shock to me too, but apparently Jimmy made a lot of investments over the years and they paid off because he left me plenty. So, don't worry, I am totally taken care of and Sam knows a lot more about running things than I do."

Vicky seemed suddenly mollified. Her whole mood appeared to shift, which Charlie had come to realize was just part of her personality. "Well, that's something. And hey if you aren't running things then that means you've got the freedom to get out of here. Maybe we could travel. Wouldn't it be fun to go on a cruise together?"

"Uh, maybe. I mean that sounds like fun, but I can't just leave the ranch—or Sam." She laughed, and it sounded a little nervous to her ears.

"Don't be silly I'm sure you can leave for a few weeks. Besides you have to make a man miss you from time to time or they take you for granted. Trust me," Vicky said with certainty.

"Maybe at some point, but probably not now, Mom. Our relationship is still pretty new and I'm not sure how he'd feel about me going off for weeks. Plus, you know there's still a lot of work around here." Her eyes flicked to the clock and she realized she needed to get going. As it was, she'd have to run to get to the barn on time.

"But that's—"

"Listen, I have to get going now, but I'll see you tomorrow okay? Maybe we can go out for lunch." Charlie didn't give her a chance to argue. She backed towards the door as she spoke, and with the last word she hurried right out and then took off at a lope across the yard.

She'd learned it was the only way to get out of the house in a reasonable time. Otherwise, Vicky would just keep making excuses to keep her there longer. Her visits to the house had become all day events because she just couldn't leave without hurting her mother's feelings. And when her feelings were hurt, she turned on the guilt trips and Charlie caved every time.

The big double doors were closed to keep the heat in, but the small side door was open, and Sam stood framed in the doorway waiting. He made a show of checking his watch. "Just in time. Good thing for your ass." He stepped back out of the doorway and gestured her in.

The gallant gesture was ruined by the hard slap he landed across the back of her skirt and she yelped.

"My office. Now," he said firmly.

She took a few steps in that direction but then stopped and turned back. "Why are you doing this here, Sam? Why not at home?" Something about being punished in the barn always made her feel vulnerable and added an extra level of embarrassment. Even though the gate would have been locked after the men left, she still always worried someone might return.

"Because I thought you should be reminded of the work you've been shirking. You seem to have forgotten all about how you wanted to help run things and wanted to learn how to do everything. I've been patient about all the time with your mother—"

She opened her mouth to protest and he waved his hand sharply to silence her and then continued. "—even though I've barely seen you since she got here. And I haven't minded you not picking up much work around the ranch either, but when I actually *need* you, you better show up."

"I really meant to be here. I just lost track." She looked down and scuffed her shoe on the wooden floor. "Every time I went to leave mom would start talking about something else and I just forgot."

"That's been happening a lot. Like almost every day," Sam pointed out. The sternness in his voice didn't lessen.

She sighed. "It's exciting hearing all about her life. Telling her about mine. I really feel like we're getting to be close and it's nice after all these years."

"And in the meantime, I barely see you, you don't show up to work, and you never even filled out the paperwork to start the spring semester for the classes you were going to take. It feels like you've put your whole life on hold for someone who never bothered to come around until now."

That hurt and she flinched. When he put it like that, yes, it did seem like she'd sort of dumped everything in her life for Vicky. "But Jimmy was the one who kept her from coming around, Sam. You can't blame her for that," she had to point out.

"That's what she *says* yeah, but we don't know the whole story, do we?" He reached out and lifted her chin with two fingers. "Charlie, I do understand your excitement. I really do. But you can't just drop your own life to keep her entertained."

She blew out a frustrated breath. "I know it's just … it's really hard to pull away from her. She gets very persistent."

"Then maybe this reminder will give you incentive to cut her off. You're not a kid Charlie, you don't need her permission to leave, but I am your Dom, and you *do* need to listen to me. Now, get your butt to the office." He let go of her, turned her around and sent her with another sharp smack that had her yelping.

"That's what I get for wearing a skirt," she muttered.

"You sure have been wearing a lot of them lately. I kind of like the easy access," Sam commented with a laugh. He followed her down the main aisle to the back of the barn where his office was.

She gritted her teeth and muttered again, much quieter. She hated skirts except on rare occasions and those usually involved going someplace fancy. Otherwise, she found pants more comfortable, especially jeans. They fit her lifestyle a heck of a lot better too, since she spent so much time working on the ranch. At least she had until her mother had arrived.

And the sudden skirt trend was courtesy of Vicky too. Vicky had hinted repeatedly that she didn't find Charlie's more casual wardrobe very ladylike. It had started as just the occasional comment about how nice she'd look in a dress, but eventually Vicky had taken advantage of their shopping trips to insist she try some on.

Of course, once she saw Charlie in the skirt or dress it was inevitable that she'd insist her daughter needed it because it was *'just perfect'*. So now she had a whole bunch of skirts and dresses that she hated, and when she went up to the main house in anything else Vicky complained.

On one level it disturbed her how much her lifestyle was changing since her mother arrived. It wasn't just the clothes; that was annoying, but she could deal with that. It was the other stuff that bothered her more.

She missed working on the ranch. She missed spending time with the animals and of course she missed Sam the most. Often by the time she got back to the house Sam had already fixed himself something to eat so she lost that time with him. Bedtime came early so there were plenty of nights when she found him getting ready for sleep when she came home.

She kept promising to be home early and she always ended up breaking those promises. So far, he'd been pretty understanding about the situation, but she had a feeling that they were coming to an end on that. She wasn't sure what to do because it felt like she was going to be stuck between the man she loved and the mom she'd been waiting for all her life.

None of this was anything she wanted to confess to Sam who would take it all as evidence that there was a problem with Vicky being there. And that wasn't the worst she had to confess either. She'd lied to him. Well, more evaded, but he'd consider it a lie.

The date construction was supposed to start had passed a couple of days before and she'd let him think the delay was on their part—another project running over deadline that had to be finished first. The truth was a *little* different. She'd explained that they had a houseguest and that, of course, they weren't canceling the work, but she wouldn't mind if they finished up other things first.

She hadn't technically rescheduled. She'd just told them that she was flexible and that she wouldn't mind if they didn't rush over. The company had been happy to bump her back on the list. She was hoping that everything would come together, and she'd never have to admit that to Sam.

She stopped at the threshold of the office, unwilling to face the music, but Sam planted a hand on her back and gave her a gentle push inside the room.

He didn't wait for her to come up with excuses but got right down to business. "You know what to do." He jerked his chin towards the beat-up old desk.

Charlie sighed and bit down on her bottom lip as she crossed the office to stand in front of it. She slowly leaned over and planted her hands flat on the top, which wasn't what he wanted, and she knew it. But she kind of loved it when he got impatient and positioned her the way he wanted her—even though she knew it would probably add to the punishment in one way or another.

He came up behind her and pressed until she was flat on the desk with her cheek against the wooden surface. His body molded to hers as he bent to whisper in her ear. "You're not doing yourself any favors, girl. I've been itching to wear out your ass for a few days now. You really want to push on this?"

"No..." Maybe she did though because she wiggled her ass, grinding back against him playfully. She really had missed him, missed their nightly playtime. It wasn't punishment she was wanting right now.

Unfortunately, punishment was what she'd earned, and Sam wasn't going to let her change course this time. "No, Charlie. Nice try, but no. This little discussion is long overdue. You're not turning this into sex." His whisper had grown harsher by the end.

He straightened and yanked her skirt up onto her back roughly. "If you're going to keep behaving like this, I might just keep you in skirts. Sure makes this easier," he commented. He dropped her underwear so fast they landed on the floor before she even realized what was happening.

She heard the icy chill of anger in his voice and suddenly she wondered if this was really just because of a missed shift. It seemed like there was something bigger going on. She shifted a little, craning her head to look back over her shoulder so she could try to gauge his level of annoyance.

"Eyes front, Charlotte. If I see your face again, I'm going to start adding to the punishment."

Charlotte? He almost never used her full name. That wasn't good at all.

Her head snapped back around without needing any further inducement. "Sam, I'm really sorry I missed work. I promise it won't happen again," she assured him with all the sincerity she could muster. It had been a while since she'd been in really deep trouble.

Since things had started running smoothly there had been discipline for small things, and the playful kind of punishment that they both could enjoy, nothing major. But she was starting to think she'd drastically underestimated how much trouble she was in.

"What did you call me? Am I Sam when you're being punished?"

She really was making everything worse. "Sorry, Daddy. I meant Daddy." He hadn't had to remind her of that in ages because she's started doing it as a matter of habit, but she was so anxious her mind wasn't really engaged.

"I forgive you, Charlie. I'm adding another five with the belt though, because you obviously need it." His large, calloused hand settled on her bare ass cheek and squeezed hard. "Grab the desk, girl. I'm done giving reminders today so any mistakes will have instant penalties," he warned her.

She expected him to start with his hand. Even when he was punishing her, he almost always did. It was a warmup, but only in the way that sitting on a hotplate was a warmup for dunking your butt in lava—Sam had a hard and heavy hand. But they both liked the more personal touch of skin-to-skin to start with. It eased them into the scene.

So, when she heard the belt whistling through the loops she shivered, but she wasn't actually expecting to feel the evil sting right then. She thought maybe he was going to put it in front of her so she could be reminded of what was coming. Or possibly he just wanted to have it ready and waiting.

She was taken completely by surprise a second later when a searing line of fire slashed across her ass and sent her up on her toes with a startled yelp of pain. She was half-way to rising from the desk before she remembered his warning and threw herself flat again.

"Daddy! That hurt!" she blurted. It was embarrassing and clichéd to say it and she regretted the lapse before the last syllable left her lips, but the surprise had been completely unpleasant.

"Pretty sure it's meant to, kid, unless the point of punishment has changed recently. Since you're feeling talkative though, you might as well count them out as we do this. I know how much you love that." He snickered a little because she hated having to keep track of the numbers and he knew it.

She felt like stomping her feet and banging her fists against the desk, but she reined herself in and had to be satisfied with letting her forehead thump solidly against the desktop. "One," she mumbled.

"Good girl. I'm not feeling like stopping after every stroke to wait around for you to remember to count so we're going to blaze through this quickly. Make sure you keep up."

A shudder went down her back and a slight moan of dismay slipped out too softly for him to hear. The belt brought a fierce sting with it but there was something almost sensual about the burning caress of leather across her skin. Even during punishment her body often reacted with arousal when he used leather – at least for a while.

That wasn't the case when the belt strokes came fast, and it sounded like that was his plan. This wasn't going to be any fun at all.

He began to swing the leather, snapping it across her ass with broad strokes. There was barely a second between them as he layered lines of fire on top of each other before slowly shifting his aim to untouched areas.

The only way she could keep up with the counting was to say them out the second the belt crashed down, almost like she was using the momentum of the swing to push the numbers out. It worked for a while but by the time she got to twenty she was struggling to keep up.

"Twenty—Daddy please! Twenty-one! Please, I'm sorry!" It was her own fault she was getting behind because she kept trying to plead with him between the strokes and there just wasn't enough time.

"You're falling behind, girl. If I don't hear that number before the next one lands, it's just going to be a bonus." He didn't even pause while he warned her, and the belt slashed down across her bare ass four more times just while he was saying it.

It left her uncertain of what number to count since she hadn't been able to count any of those, but he helped her out. "Start with twenty-five."

She appreciated that those weren't extras, but there was something ominous about the way he said it that made her wonder how long this was going to go on. Her tolerance for pain was high and she could play for hours when she was in the right mood and with slow preparation.

But this was punishment. There was nothing sexy about it and there had been no slow building of heat, so she was finding herself already close to tears. She was struggling to hold them back when she counted thirty and surprisingly, he stopped. As tempting as it was to look back over her shoulder, she didn't dare.

"You got anything extra you want to confess while we're doing this? Anything you might feel guilty for?" he asked pointedly.

The way he said it made her wonder if he already knew what she'd done. It felt like she was being led into a trap, but she couldn't be sure. "N-no Daddy. Nothing important." She was going to regret lying and she knew it, but it slipped out before she really thought it over.

There was an ominous silence, and it made her twitchy. She tried to stay still but every time he moved, she flinched in anticipation of another smack. Finally, it came, a hard strike to her right cheek with the flat of his hand. It stayed there, holding the heat against her skin and squeezing the rounded flesh until she squirmed.

"Do you know why I'm so pissed at you right now, Charlie?"

She sniffled and jerked her head in a quick negative. "I guess 'cause I've been ignoring you a lot lately?"

"I'm not mad because you're all wrapped up in forming a relationship with your mom. I get that. I'm not mad because you've been blowing off everything else—annoyed, but not mad. No, what has me absolutely furious right now is that I thought we were past you sneaking around behind my back."

Her insides did a queasy roll and her ass tightened reflexively with fear. She realized it had been stupid of her to think that Sam wouldn't know she'd put off the work on the house. She'd known it was a mistake not to tell him from the start, but she'd gone with 'better to ask forgiveness than permission' and went right ahead anyway.

Now she was really in for it. "I'm sorry, Daddy. I swear I didn't think it was a big deal. I thought it would be okay." That was another lie and an obvious one so there was no surprise when his hand swept up and then crashed down across her left cheek with enough force that she cried out.

"You didn't think it would be a big deal? Really?" His tone was absolutely frigid, and she knew if she looked back his eyes would be ice.

"I mean, okay I knew you'd be annoyed but I didn't think you'd be *this* mad." She sniffled and pulled a little tighter into herself. "It's just been hard trying to please both of you and I thought it would be easier if—"

He interrupted her with a growl. "You didn't think at all, Charlie. If you had, you would have known this was a huge deal. Not only did you break the rules and go behind my back, but you broke our trust too and I'm not even sure what you thought you were going to accomplish." The harsh tones had softened towards the end and there was a note of confusion and hurt there. "I want to know why you'd do this."

He was so upset, and it was her fault. Her chest tightened making it hard for her to breathe and tears started to roll down her cheeks. The beginning signs of a panic attack were lurking.

She was messing things up again. She hadn't meant to. It hadn't seemed like a huge deal. She'd figured letting fate decide when the work would start was a fair compromise. Her legs trembled as she tried to calm herself. She'd expected a punishment when he found out, because she'd gone against him, but she hadn't expected anything like this.

"I—I know I shouldn't have, Daddy. I'm really sorry," she whispered.

"The worst thing about all of this Charlie is that I really don't understand why you'd do it. I thought this ranch was important to you. I thought you wanted to help me run things. We had big plans together, so I just don't get it."

Now it was her turn to be confused and she pushed herself up on her elbows and half turned to look at him. The consequences of getting up without permission were the last thing on her mind. "Wait... Sam, you know the ranch means everything to me. Besides you it's the most important thing in my life. Spending time with my mom and holding up the construction to keep her comfortable has nothing to do with that."

He just stared at her. The anger dropped away and left confusion in its place. "Charlie ... this isn't about your mom or the construction." He paused and frowned. "Though I guess we're going to be talking about that one too."

She realized in that moment she'd just ratted herself out and could only sigh, but that left her completely unsure of what he was talking about. "I don't understand. If that's not why you're mad then what did I do? As far as I know that's the only rule I've broken lately."

His eyes narrowed and he was silent as he searched her expression, probably looking for a sign of guilt, but she was being honest. She had no clue.

"I'm talking about you calling around, asking if anyone was interested in buying the ranch, Charlie."

"What?" She could feel her face twisting with shock. "Seriously, Sam?" She pushed herself up off the desk and turned so she could look at him directly.

He frowned but didn't say anything about it. He was more concerned with what was happening. "I was told today that you had called several different spreads in the area and were feeling out their interest in acquiring this ranch. Either the whole thing, or in pieces."

She shook her head firmly. Now she knew she was in the clear, at least on this one. "No way. I would never do that. I'm never going to sell the ranch and even if I wanted to, I don't think I can until I get my degree. And even then, we'll both be equal owners, so you'd have to agree anyway."

"You're sure about that? You need to be real sure, girl, because this is serious."

"C'mon, does that sound like me? Okay, yes, I went behind your back about selling some of the fields sure, but that was for a plan. You know I wouldn't sell the whole ranch. I'd never do that."

The tension began to leave his body slowly. The deep lines around his mouth and eyes smoothed out and he nodded. "You're right. I thought back to the last time and it felt similar, so I thought…"

"Last time was before we worked things out. I wouldn't dare do that now unless I wanted my ass busted. Besides I only ever wanted to sell the grass fields because I thought it would be more efficient to buy the hay than work them ourselves. I wanted to make the ranch better, not sell it off," she pointed out.

That seem to assuage the last of his suspicions and he pulled her into his arms. "You're right." He frowned. "I'm not sure exactly what's going on, but I believe you. I'm sorry, darlin'." His mouth came down on hers with a fierceness that took her by surprise, but her body responded immediately.

She hadn't gone to the barn expecting to have sex on his desk but somehow that was what ended up happening. It was fast and raw with passion. The location wasn't ideal for either of them. It was especially uncomfortable for her, since her sore hot ass was rubbing against the hard surface of the desk every time he thrust into her.

But it was also satisfying in a way she couldn't explain.

The best sex always seemed to come after a fight, and while this hadn't exactly been a fight there *had* been a building of emotions on both sides that needed to come out somehow. She couldn't imagine how betrayed Sam must have felt to think she was trying to sell the ranch out from under him. That was something they were going to need to discuss in further detail when they could both think again.

But in that moment, she just wanted to lose herself in pleasure. Her eyes closed and the noise in the small room seemed to magnify until it became a background soundtrack of moans and rasping breaths, punctuated by the meaty sounds of his body slapping up against hers. It was raw and primal and exactly what they needed.

She wrapped her legs around his waist and rocked her hips to take him deeper. It was just on the edge of being too much, but somehow perfect and when he hit the right spot her whole body tensed without warning as a wave of intense pleasure rolled through her. She tightened around his shaft and he groaned.

"You're mine, girl, and we're not even close to being done yet." The words were harsh and ragged with exertion.

She opened her eyes to see the concentration on his face as he deliberately held back his own orgasm so he could continue to invade her body with one long thrust after another. There was no complaint from her, not when she could already feel her body shifting gears to build towards another round of pleasure.

She loved Sam with all her heart, but at moments like this she felt like she was completely claimed by him and that she didn't even have words for. It was everything.

CHAPTER 8

When Charlie didn't show up, he was pissed. He tried calling her cell, but she didn't answer. No doubt she'd forgotten her phone at home when she went up to the big house. He didn't have the time to run up there and grab her. They were short staffed, so he had to put off his own work to take the place he'd slotted her for.

That she was going to get her butt whupped was a done deal as far as he was concerned, but by the time he came back from the winter pasture, and got his horse settled down in her stall he'd calmed down about it. He'd worked some of the frustration out of his system and he'd gone back to reminding himself that this was all new to Charlie and she was just obsessed at the moment.

He was sure she'd break out of it eventually. He was more concerned with the changes he'd noted in his girl. He'd met Vicky a couple of times now, and she hadn't impressed him much. Maybe it was Mike's words influencing his opinion, but he sensed something shady and deceptive about Charlie's mother. As far as he was concerned the sooner she hit the road the better.

But until she was gone, he was doing his best to support Charlie's desire to form a relationship with her—while still keeping her feet on the ground. That meant he was going to be patient and understanding, but he was still going to punish her for not following through on her responsibilities.

All that patience went out the window when the phone in his office rang. It was an old school landline, and the unit itself had probably been on the wall since before he'd been born, at least it looked like it. These days most business was routed to his cell but every now and then someone would call direct and the sudden raucous sound would send him shooting out of his chair with his heart racing.

"For fuck's sake!" he snarled as he grabbed for the handset with its mile-long coiling cord. "You've got Sam Mason here." He made an attempt to sound professional because he knew it was likely something to do with the ranch.

But he wasn't expecting the conversation that followed, and it was a conversation that would end up being repeated twice more that morning. The other at least came by cell, so they didn't knock ten years off his life each time, but that didn't make them much easier to deal with.

What the hell was Charlie up to this time?

He could barely even credit what he'd been told, but the repetition had certainly helped it to sink in. It was a struggle to wait until the end of the day when everyone left before he went to hunt her up. He knew he was going to want privacy for the conversation he was about to have with his bratty little girl. He also needed some time to cool down before he fetched her, because he was not only furious but hurt too.

Each time the story was repeated he felt like he'd been stabbed in the gut. He didn't see how it could be a mistake, but he still hoped it was. Maybe she'd be able to explain it, but one thing he knew was this was a discussion for the barn not their home.

Once everyone was gone for the day, he headed off to get her. He knew where she'd be, of course. As soon as he saw her sitting alone in the kitchen, he forgot about the fact that her mother would be around. Charlie got all of his focus, but he had no intention of telling her that he knew.

He'd bring that up at the right time. He wanted to see if she'd lie about it, but for now the missed shift would be enough reason to call her to the barn.

When Vicky popped up suddenly it was irritating and he didn't like the way she tried to override him, but he accepted that as Charlie's mother a little of that would be natural. But then the woman had dismissed him as a hired hand with such disdain.

He didn't really think of himself as better than the other people who worked the ranch. They were a team. So, if she wanted to consider him just a hand, he wasn't going to quibble about it. It was the heavy disgust in her voice that bothered him. Like he was trash. He saw in that moment exactly what Mike did, and elitist snob didn't even begin to cover it.

For just one second, he actually pictured himself putting the mother, and not the daughter, across his knee to knock some of that uppity attitude out of her system. He'd never do it, of course, but the thought was incredibly tempting.

He also didn't say any of the nasty things that were right on the tip of his tongue. It was all he could do to shut the woman out and leave Charlie with a warning to be on time for their discussion. His tone made it clear that being late would be a big mistake and then he left before he could make a mistake of his own.

He had a feeling Charlie would find a way to make it to the barn on time and she did, barely. He had calmed down from earlier in the day and was no longer as furious, but the hurt was still there. It made him want to be harsh with her, though he held back on those instincts.

She didn't seem to realize what was wrong. Her decision to try to sell the ranch, or even entertain offers, without talking to him first wasn't a minor thing. It wasn't something he could just spank her for and then move on.

It was a relationship-shaking problem. He could, and would, punish her for the part where she broke the rules they'd set up, but that wasn't going to solve the root issue. The ranch had been their dream, not just hers. What did it mean for their relationship if she no longer wanted to be part of it?

Hell, even further what did that mean for his whole life, which he'd built around working the spread. As half owner he was pretty sure he could keep it from being sold, even if the lawyer didn't say no, but then what? He couldn't see them settling easily back into the relationship they'd built with such a huge issue between them.

Things had been going so well, and now this. It took a real effort for him to push those concerns back so he could deal with the missing work first. It was a much smaller problem, but the punishment would break down some of her walls.

That would prime her for dealing with the real issue. Charlie struggled less after she'd been punished. But even sniffling and with a sore butt he hadn't expected her to just admit it like it was unimportant.

"I'm sorry, Daddy. I swear I didn't think it was a big deal. I thought it would be okay." She said it in her little girl being punished voice, the one that usually tugged at all his heartstrings. This time it just compounded the hurt. How could she think it was okay?

It turned out she hadn't thought it was okay, because she was innocent—the little side issue of her confused confession to something else was another matter. But as soon as they'd started talking it through and cleared up the confusion on both sides it became obvious that she was telling the truth.

He wondered how he could ever have believed she'd try to sell the ranch. It was so far off from anything she'd ever wanted ... except lately she'd barely been interested. Her mother was definitely against the place and made it plain that she could hardly stand to be as close to it as she was in the main house. So, in the back of his mind, he'd wondered if this was another one of the many changes he'd noticed in her lately.

Still, suddenly wearing dresses all the time was one thing, wanting to change the whole course of her life was something else. He should have realized something was off. He still couldn't explain the situation. People he'd known and trusted for years couldn't all be spontaneously lying to him.

And why would they bother anyway? There was no point to it. The mystery had him reeling.

But he still felt guilty for assuming it was true. It was nothing compared to the relief of finding out it was a lie though, and at least he hadn't just stormed in and whupped her ass for something she hadn't done. He didn't usually do things like that, but he'd been pretty damn tempted after the third call.

He wasn't sure he'd have been able to drop the guilt of that.

But the relief had been so strong that he grabbed her and kissed her hard, just needing to claim her physically. From there it had turned into a bout of wild fucking on his creaky old desk. It wasn't planned. It just happened. The sparks and fire shifted and the next thing he knew he was sliding between her sweet thighs and plunging home.

It had always been like this between them. Back when they had dated before, almost every fight had ended up twisting into rough sex. And now, as he thrust deep into her and she moaned his name, he was reminded of those days. He didn't want to go back to the constant chaos and arguing, but he couldn't deny the passion still stirred them up.

They needed this, both of them. Right now, every other problem in the world disappeared. All he could think about was her soft skin and the way she felt when she tightened around his cock, like she was trying to drain him dry.

She came, but that wasn't enough for him. It only whetted his appetite for more. He wanted to bring her to the point of begging. He wanted to empty her mind so that nothing existed but him. His hips snapped forward steadily, thrusting like a piston in an engine until she began to writhe and whimper under him with another building climax.

But it was too soon for that. He wanted this to last for both of them and knew he wouldn't be able to hold out if she came again. He drove her to the edge and then pulled back. The moaning developed a whining tone to it as he left her primed and ready, but never quite there. Every time one of them came close he shifted his rhythm or paused to let it recede.

"Don't come, baby!" The order was snapped, harsh and her reply was a long whimper of need. "If you come before I say you can, you won't sit for a week, Charlie." The warning had her biting down on her bottom lip and giving him desperate pleading stares, which he ignored.

Every gasp, every moan drove him crazy. It took every trick in the book to keep from coming, but then her voice began to rise as she chanted 'uh uh uh please pleaseeeee'. He pulled on the last of his self-control and forced himself to freeze in mid-stroke.

Her eyes opened, filled with confusion. Her lips parted to ask why he stopped but he cut her off. His voice was harsh. "Beg me, Darlin'. Beg for what you want, or I'll stop right now." The order was nearly a snarl dredged up from deep in his need to finish. To push her further along, he reached down and began to circle her clit with the pad of his thumb, and she reacted with a squirm that almost ruined it all.

There was zero chance he would have stopped at that point. He wasn't even sure he could have, but it didn't matter since she complied with desperation. "Please Daddy, don't stop. I need to come, please *please*." The words were interrupted with pants and little sounds of her rising pleasure and that alone was enough to drive him over the edge.

He grabbed her hips in a harsh grip, pinned her in place as he forced back the tide long enough to get in a few more strokes. "Come, Charliegirl. Come for Daddy." He shifted, ever so slightly, to stroke in just the right spot and suddenly her whole body arched up off the desk with a pure animal wail.

He'd never known a woman as reactive as Charlie. Sometimes her dramatics in the throes of passion were over the top, but she wasn't faking anything. It wasn't the first time he'd been glad they didn't have any close neighbors, except the horses. They were probably stamping restlessly, but at least they wouldn't gossip about it.

When her walls tightened around him this time, there was no chance of holding back. He managed one more half-hearted thrust, holding it for an endless moment, and then collapsed forward across her body with a groan. The desk creaked ominously and for a second he was sure it was just going to quit in disgust and dump both of them on the ground.

But after a second of tension, it became clear that it was going to survive their encounter. Charlie laughed, a sound of pure mirth without the accompanying tension that had so often been there recently. He couldn't resist leaning in to catch the last of it by covering her lips with his.

As much as he would have liked to have stay there, nestled between her thighs, still joined to her body, the desk was just about the most uncomfortable place they could have chosen for this. And he was already starting to get a cramp from the awkward height. With a sigh he pushed himself off of her. His half-soft shaft slipped from her body and she sighed as she looked up at him.

"It would be nice if all punishment ended like this."

He snorted, giving her a look. "It's not punishment if it ends like this and you know it." There were things he needed to say, but he needed time to get his thoughts in order. They were still spiraling, and he took a moment to fix his clothes and help her off the desk.

They both looked respectable once she was standing. Her skirt slid down conveniently to cover the nakedness underneath and only the underwear on the floor would have given them away. He snatched those up and handed them to her before they were forgotten. *Wouldn't **that** be a fun conversation to have with one of the hands?*

"Yeah..." She sighed again as she took her crumpled panties from him and stepped into them. A few wiggles and they were back in place and everything looked perfectly innocent.

Although when he looked, he could see her pupils were still blown and her lips swollen from the hard kisses. It was a subtle kind of evidence, but it was there, at least to his eyes. "Today was a one shot, because well, I was an asshole for being pissed before I even talked with you. And I stewed in my own juices all day so finding out it wasn't true pushed me into a whole other headspace, darlin'."

"You do believe me then? I mean I'm kind of shocked you thought I'd even consider selling but ..."

"I believe you and yeah, I should have known. But we've got a big mystery on our hands and I want it solved fast." He reached out, tucking a stray strand of hair back behind her ear. His knuckles caressed the line of her cheek gently. "Let's go home and talk about this."

The horses were restless, probably from all the noise she'd been making either during the spanking or the sex that followed, but it didn't take long to reassure the most anxious animals and close up the barn for the night. They held hands on the way back to the house and there was a peaceful silence between them.

The punishment and quickie in the office had at least dissolved some of the frustration he'd been feeling and that was something. He had a feeling it wasn't going to last, so he took the time to enjoy it. The air was chilled with the oncoming winter, which didn't encourage him to draw out the walk, as much as he was tempted to delay the conversation they needed to have.

It had warmed up briefly after the early freeze, but the temperatures had dropped again steadily, and he stopped to grab an armload of firewood on the way inside. They would need the emotional comfort of a fire.

"Why don't you fix us something to eat, while I get the fire going, Charlie?" It was phrased as a question, but the tone made it clear he was giving her an order. He hadn't forgotten her inadvertent confession earlier and wanted to make it clear that it was also on the agenda for their discussion.

She picked up the cue. "Yes Daddy." Without complaint she went straight to the fridge and poked her head in. "We're low on groceries but we have eggs and bacon. Feel like a breakfast for dinner meal?" She sounded guilty. While cooking had been her suggestion, grocery shopping was an · assigned chore since her schedule was more flexible than his —she'd been slacking on both.

But breakfast suited him fine. "Sounds good to me."

Crouched in front of the fireplace he settled a couple of logs on the bottom and stuffed old newspapers and dried pinecones between and under them. It only took a minute or so to get a decent flame going. He stood up, brushed his hands off on his jeans and eyed it critically to make sure it was going to keep burning.

Once he'd decided it was going well enough not to need supervision, he joined her in the kitchen area. He wrapped an arm around her waist and snugged her back against his body as she started laying strips of bacon in the frying pan. "I'm going to take a quick shower and wash the sweat off." The words were softly spoken next to her ear and followed with a kiss.

She melted back against him with a happy sigh. "Don't take too long, it should be done in ten minutes or so."

He didn't make it a long shower, but it was an extra hot one. By the time he'd washed off the day's sweat and changed into a pair of baggy pajama bottoms the whole house smelled like sizzling bacon and his stomach grumbled. He heard the toaster pop just as he left the bedroom and considered it perfect timing.

Over dinner it was like having his old Charlie back, the pre-Vicky Charlie who he could talk to while they ate. His girl who laughed and smiled, and sometimes sat in his lap so he could feed her bites off his plate. Had it really only been weeks? It felt like so much longer that there'd been this strain between them.

He wanted to hold onto the moment. It was going to get worse before it got better because he could see now that Vicky had her hooks in deep. That was a problem because it had occurred to him in the shower that the most likely suspect of trying to sell the ranch ... was Charlie's mother.

Vicky hated the ranch and always had. She'd settled into the main house and suddenly Charlie barely set foot on the working property. She didn't visit the animals, she didn't go riding, and she'd even missed work shifts.

So, if there was a woman calling around about trying to sell the ranch, well, he couldn't think of anyone else who had a motive. And of course, since Vicky had lived here a ways back, she probably remembered the other ranchers in the area, which also gave her opportunity. But he could have caught the woman posting a for sale sign on the front gate and Charlie *still* wouldn't want to hear that her mother was probably to blame.

He didn't know how she thought she'd get away with it, or what she was trying to accomplish by doing it, but his instincts told him that Vicky was responsible.

As Charlie shifted into his lap and snuggled up, he realized that he didn't have the energy to bring that up with her —not tonight. He needed to suggest her mother might be responsible in a way that wouldn't immediately make her defensive. They needed to discuss it, but there were other things to talk about too, and all of it would be too much after the long day.

He squeezed her tight. "So, little girl, you made a confession earlier. You want to tell me about that?"

She tilted her head back and looked up at him with a frown. "Not really? I mean, if it's a choice I'd rather not."

He laughed and smacked her ass lightly. "Sorry, did phrasing it as a question confuse you? It's not a choice. Spit it out."

Her bottom lip pouted, and she let out a long dramatic sigh. "Well ... you said you wanted the work to start in two weeks."

"Charlie, I know what *I* said. Let's move along to the part where it didn't start and why."

She muttered something under her breath about how she was getting to that, but before he needed to encourage her, she continued. "Vicky was just talking about how she's got dust allergies—apparently that was one of the reasons she never liked the ranch. All the dust drove her crazy."

He patted her ass in warning. Hearing Vicky's life story wasn't really necessary. She was stalling and they both knew it.

"Well, I told her we'd have them start downstairs and she could stay in the upstairs part as long as she needed ... but she was worried about the dust and well ..."

When she didn't continue, he growled. "Well, what?"

"Well, I said that I couldn't move the construction because we might lose our spot. You know because with winter coming, they have to get as much work—"

"Charlie." This time it was punctuated with a hard swat that made her yelp and jump in his lap. "I know how construction schedules work. Finish the story."

With big round eyes, full of false innocence she finally spit out the rest. "So, I called them and said that we weren't rescheduling, but that we were fine with delays on their end if they had other projects to finish first."

"I see."

Her glance dropped to her hands, twisting around each other in her lap. "I figured it wouldn't really make much of a difference because if they finished other things then they'd have more crew to work on this all at once. So maybe the timing would end up about the same," she explained.

That was pretty much never how it worked with construction, but he'd give her the benefit on that one. "So, if you thought it would be fine then why didn't you talk to me first?"

"I just thought you might be annoyed because I know you've been worried about Vicky staying around." Her voice was so low he had to lean in to hear it.

"You didn't want me to know her visit was going to be a lot longer than we expected?"

"No—I mean kind of. I don't know for sure that it *will* be longer. She hasn't really said." She wasn't meeting his eyes.

"But you think that's what it means?"

"Yes, Daddy."

He sighed. "You know why I'm worried about her being here, Charlie. You know what Mike said too. Did you ever go talk to him about it?"

She shook her head and he put two fingers under her chin and forced it up so he could see her face. "Why not?"

"I just … I don't know. Maybe she's different now. It's been a long time. I get that she was a bitch to Mike back then and she made a lot of mistakes, but that was soooo many years ago. He hasn't seen her since then, so he only knows who she *was*." The words were hesitant, nervous, like she was trying to convince herself just as much as him.

She wasn't wrong though. People did change. He had. "People change but they also have baggage that they carry with them, Charlie. Knowing about her history would let you see if she really has changed or if she's still the person she was. I can't help feeling like you're afraid to find out the truth on this one."

Her shoulders shook and she nodded, just once. He wasn't sure if it was in agreement or just acknowledging what he'd said. She slid around, straddling him and letting her legs hang down on either side of the chair as her head tucked into the hollow of his neck. "I should have talked to you," she admitted.

"Yep." His arms wrapped around her, holding her tight to his chest.

"Am I in trouble?"

"Yep. But since you just got my belt across your ass for missing your shift, I think I'll sort out another kind of punishment for this. I think we need something that will make the lesson stick for longer than it takes for you to sit comfortably." He wasn't sure exactly what that would be. Some chores would probably be part of it, but he'd figure out the whole thing later.

He wanted to relax and just enjoy holding her in his lap, but his mind wouldn't stop working through the problem they *hadn't* discussed yet. He wondered if Charlie would bring up the reports that she was selling the ranch before he did. She had to be curious about it too, but she seemed content so relax in his lap.

Well, he didn't intend to mention her mother tonight, but he had to at least talk about the calls. "Charlie? Can you think of any explanation for why three people would call to ask me about you selling the ranch?"

Her body stiffened, and her arms around his neck tightened. "I don't know, Sam. I just know it wasn't me." She paused, and then like she was afraid to ask the question, "What did they say exactly?"

"Well, Jim Musgrave wanted to know if I was looking for work since you were selling. When I said you weren't selling, he was confused, said he got a call from you a few days back asking if he was interested in expanding." That had been the earliest call. At first, he'd been sure it had to be a mistake.

"I haven't seen Jim since before college. I doubt he'd even recognize my voice," she pointed out.

That was a point in her favor, but not in Vicky's. "I asked if he knew about anyone else getting a call like that. Said I thought maybe someone was playing a trick, and he said he'd look into it. Pete Jones and Serilda Bailey heard from him I was asking so they both called me direct to say they'd gotten the calls too."

"Well, Pete … I don't know, Sam. He knows me but it's been a while. I can't say he'd recognize my voice and I don't even know anyone named Serilda." Charlie finally pushed herself back so she could look him in the eyes.

"Serilda bought out Matthew a couple years back. She's his ex-wife. You'll remember him because he used to team up with your father for harvest season sometimes." She nodded; Matthew was hard to forget. He was a big man with a bigger laugh that could practically shake the walls and he'd been around a lot when they were kids. "Well, when they got divorced, he decided it was time to retire. His arthritis had gotten pretty bad and he wanted to move someplace warm, so she bought him out."

"Well, he'd have recognized my voice, but I never met her. I guess it could have been any woman using my name and they wouldn't have known." She gave him a nervous look as though afraid he'd start suspecting her again and then sighed. "Do you think it *was* a prank? Someone just trying to be funny?"

"Maybe." No, he didn't. But it was possible, barely, that it could be.

"I don't really understand why anyone would do it. I mean what's the point?" She frowned and he could see the wheels turning. For a second he almost thought she was going to make the connection, but then she burrowed back against him.

He held her like that a little longer, but the hard chair wasn't comfortable so pretty soon they moved into the living room to snuggle up in front of the fire. Despite all the problems of the day, and the worries on his mind, he enjoyed the time, and he was reluctant to get up and disturb her, but as the fire died down, he sighed and stretched carefully under her body.

She was half asleep by then anyway. She mumbled something he couldn't understand in a drowsy voice as he lifted her and carried her into the bedroom. She looked beautiful curled up on the sheets with her hair loose and spilling around her face and he was struck with a sudden possessive feeling. *Mine!*

The idea that anyone would take her away made his insides clench painfully. He really was worried about Vicky. He sensed a predator in her. She wanted something from Charlie and she wasn't going to leave until she got it. His biggest concern was that what she wanted might be for Charlie to leave with her.

If it had been something as simple as another man coming around, he would have gone in swinging, but this wasn't that kind of fight. He couldn't chase Vicky off like she was a coyote after the herd. All he could do was try to influence Charlie to step back, guard her feelings, and try not to get sucked in.

Course he'd already done that and so far, it hadn't gone well. He sighed as he climbed in beside her and pulled her back against him. He buried his face in her hair and inhaled the sweet smell of strawberries from the shampoo she used. The scent of her relaxed him.

He was bone tired and he wanted to sleep, but his mind kept whirling, looking for solutions to his problems. Most of them seemed, at least at the moment, unsolvable, but he did at least work out her punishment before he finally dropped off much later than normal.

When the alarm went off just a few hours later, he was tempted to shut it off and go back to sleep. His second was experienced and would cover if he wasn't there. Now and then it did happen that he was late for some reason and when that occurred, Ben had always stepped in to parcel out the assignments with no lapse in authority.

Sometimes Sam wondered if he couldn't step back from such a heavy schedule and let Ben take over more responsibilities. The older man knew what he was doing and could easily run things without Sam, but it wasn't really his style to let other people shoulder his work, so he sat up and yawned.

Next to him Charlie had somehow managed to steal most of the covers, and yet still her leg from foot to thigh was bare and exposed. He reached over and settled his hand on her warm skin at the ankle and then slid it all the way up to her ass. He gave one cheek a gentle squeeze and then he followed it up with a hard smack that made it bounce.

It startled her awake and she rolled over wide-eyed. "What!"

He tucked away the grin at her shocked response. "Time to get up, kid."

She squinted; a look of confusion crossed her face. "Wait... why? I'm not working today." She could also have pointed out that she rarely went in when he did. She preferred later mornings and was usually still sleeping when he headed to the barn. Contrary to popular belief, not all ranchers were morning people and Charlie proved that.

But little girls who were being punished didn't get to stroll in after sleeping late as far as he was concerned. "You are now, yeah. You missed yesterday remember? Besides some hard work will help make up for going behind my back on the construction."

Her mouth dropped open and then snapped shut with a huffing sound. She might have argued if she'd been more awake, not that it would have done her any good.

"You've got twenty minutes to be dressed and ready to go. Or else." He didn't bother to define the 'or else'; she'd find out or she wouldn't. In the meantime, he left her pouting on the bed and went to start the coffee. As usual he'd forgotten to set it up the night before, so it took him a few minutes to get it going.

He pretended not to notice when he saw her crossing to the bathroom out of the corner of his eye, but he kept his eye on the clock. When it hit twenty after and the shower was still running, he shook his head, grabbed a long wooden spoon from the drawer and headed in to drag her out.

They were *not* on time to work, but they did get there eventually, and Charlie didn't offer any backtalk when she got her assignments even though he'd given her the shit jobs —literally.

CHAPTER 9

Charlie didn't remember falling asleep. They'd been sitting in front of the fire and she'd zoned out, happy in his arms and relaxed. Next thing she knew she was being startled awake by a blazing hard spank on her ass—which was still sore from the day before.

Confused and disoriented, she'd just stared at him when he said she was going in to work with him. She didn't bother to argue. When Sam decided something, he usually stuck to it, especially when it came to punishment. The fact that she hated early mornings was probably factored in as part of it.

She couldn't say she didn't deserve it, but that didn't mean she was happy about it. The plan for her day had involved sleeping in, and then maybe heading up to the big house for brunch with her mom after a long hot shower. Instead, she was getting a short shower so she could go out in the bitter cold morning to work.

Ugh.

She knotted her hair up to keep it dry. No sense washing it and then going out in the cold; it would freeze. But the hot water was nice, and she lost track of time as she stood in the clouds of steam and tried to wake up.

She should have taken the time limit seriously. It was just that she was enjoying the shower and didn't really think a few minutes would matter. She was often late to one place or another and Sam would growl but most of the time he didn't get too annoyed.

Things tended to be different when she was already in trouble and that had slipped her mind. Lost in the heat, the sudden blast of cool air as the bathroom door swung open caught her by surprise. It was quickly followed by an uh-oh feeling as she realized she might be in trouble. "I'm almost d—"

But by then he'd yanked back the curtain and had caught her by one arm as his free hand began to pepper her wet butt with dozens of stinging smacks. The shower was still running, and he took advantage of that, turning her to rewet the skin under the spray before giving her another round with the wooden spoon.

It stung like sitting on a fire ant hill and she screeched. There was plenty of twisting and turning as she tried to evade the burning strokes. The spoon was heavy and solid, and the laminate sealant that kept bacteria from soaking in also made it extra stingy. On top of the belt welts from the day before it was anything but pleasant.

She danced around trying to keep her backside to the shower wall so he couldn't reach it, but he just slapped the outside of her thighs, which were also tender, until she turned on her own. Her nice relaxing shower morphed into a ten-minute workout that involved bending, twisting, and running in place. It had, if nothing else, woken her up.

It was probably a good thing he kept a tight grip on her the whole time, or she might have slipped during the calisthenics. As it was, she was sniffling and spilling real tears before he finally shut off the water and helped her out. Her bottom lip was stuck in a pout, but the gentle way he dried her off did a lot to soothe her.

She tried to take the towel, but he pushed her hands away. "I'll do it," he said, as he rubbed the skin dry. He was gentle when he got to the freshly spanked spots and only patted them with a soft touch. She was grateful for that because her rump was throbbing and pulsing from the nasty spoon.

She wasn't fond of wooden implements on the best of days. Leather could be sexy, but wood was almost never anything but punishment as far as she was concerned. That spoon was going to meet its end in the fireplace one night, and she'd face the consequences for it, but it would be worth it to see it burn up.

Thinking gleefully about its destruction, combined with his gentle care, did help her calm down and by the time he set the towel aside her pout had diminished. She liked it when he took control and took care of her. In some ways it made her feel more like she belonged to him than being held down and spanked did.

So, she stood there and let her eyes drift shut as he patted her down. When he was finished, she had gotten past the attitude and was ready to behave herself again.

"Go get dressed and no more stalling. We're running late now." It sounded like he was going for stern, but the order had a loving tone underneath and she couldn't resist brushing her lips across his before she hurried to the bedroom to grab her clothes.

Starting the day off with punishment probably would have put most people in a bad mood, but for her it was settling. And she'd missed working the ranch, so it was good to have an excuse to go in, even if her mother got annoyed about her not being with her all day. Plus, she was sick of wearing dresses and skirts all the time.

There was no way she was going to work in anything but pants, but she did have a moment of regret when she slipped into jeans. A skirt would have been more comfortable; the denim rubbed harshly across the spanked skin and it chaffed.

But she buttoned them up, threw on her boots and was ready to go. Sam kindly handed her a cup of hot coffee when she came out of the bedroom. It had cream and sugar enough to cool it so she could gulp it fast before he pushed her out the door and they hurried to the warmth of the barn.

Everyone was already working, and the assignments had been given out by Ben, but Sam stepped in and rearranged a few things to make sure she had work to do. She didn't even bother pulling attitude with him when he gave her the worst job of the morning; she'd expected it.

Wheeling barrows full of horse crap out to the manure pit was zero fun, and it stunk—literally. Going in and out of the barn didn't make it any better either, though at least outside the crisp cold air kept the smell down. But she'd done it before, and she knew the routine.

Her father had made it clear from her earliest days that no job on the ranch was beneath them. Owner or hand, it all needed to be done. She still remembered how he'd explained it. "Charlie, this might be our place, and we might pay people to work for us, but we still have a responsibility to pitch in. A rancher should know every single job, big or small, on their spread. And they should be willing to do any chore no matter how unpleasant it is."

He'd made sure the lesson stuck by rotating her through all of the work, just like any other hand. Her chores had always been appropriate for her skills, and in some cases her height, but other than that she'd taken the same share of the garbage jobs that everyone got. Shoveling poop and hauling it away was just one of *many* gross jobs she'd done.

And her father had tended to enforce discipline by giving

people he was annoyed at the worst assignments too, so this wasn't even the first time she'd been punished this way. Her Daddy taking a page out of her father's book kind of amused her on some level.

She did her best to breathe through her mouth so she didn't gag and went about getting it done without complaining, the way Jimmy would have expected her to. The approving nod from Sam made it worth it when she finished up and reported back to him. It wasn't the only task he had for her and her morning was busy and long, but when they stopped for lunch, he pulled her aside.

"I know you're probably wanting to get up to see your mother, but since you tend to get distracted and lose the whole day up there, I want you to get some other things done first. Head home and start the chores in the house you've been skipping to start with."

She'd been feeling guilty about that, so she didn't even argue, only sighed and nodded. Sam wasn't a typical messy guy and he liked things neat. He usually picked up after himself as well as doing his share of the regular cleaning. She was the one who had been slacking on it, but with only three rooms it wouldn't take long.

"And then after that I want you to put some time into researching your schooling plans. You're the one who decided you wanted to go back and you're probably too late to enroll for the next semester now, but that doesn't mean you can't get things lined up." He gave her a stern look, eyes piercing as he waited to see how she'd react.

She saw her day vanishing and it was a little frustrating. She did want to get up to see her mother and knew Vicky was going to be sulky about her not showing up until later. But she honestly couldn't argue with anything he was saying. All her plans had gone into stasis since her mother had arrived. She'd just completely dropped the ball on everything and part of her was feeling relieved that Sam was taking charge.

"Yes Daddy… then can I go visit?"

He seemed to be considering. His eyes narrowed thoughtfully, but finally he gave a reluctant nod. "Yeah, then you can go and if you want to have dinner with her that's fine, but I want you home by seven. I'm done with barely seeing you for days at a time, got it?" There was a clear warning there and she had a feeling she wouldn't like the consequences if she forgot to be home on time.

Later, after she'd finished her work she stopped before she left the house and set the alarm on her phone, just to make sure. It wasn't the best visit. Vicky was mad she'd come late and seemed even more annoyed when she found out that Charlie had spent the morning working on the ranch.

"You're the owner. You don't need to do that," she complained.

Charlie definitely wasn't going to explain that she hadn't had a choice because it was punishment. She also knew that Jimmy's philosophy about how owners needed to do their share wasn't going to fly with her mother. Vicky wanted no part of any dirty ranch work, so she just tried to guide the conversation into other topics.

Her mother was pleased that Charlie was staying for dinner, right up until she suggested they go out to eat. "I'd like to Mom, but I need to go by 6:45 so there won't be time."

She was expecting more irritation and she wasn't wrong. What she wasn't expecting was for Vicky to suddenly turn cold. She was used to her mother being whiney, and at times petulant. She'd seen anger too, though only in small doses that Vicky quickly suppressed.

This was new. Her mother looked hurt and turned away from Charlie to walk into the kitchen. She was silent as she pulled groceries from the fridge and started making dinner.

Vicky didn't cook, not really. She seemed to live mostly on salads and that was what she was lining up on the counter.

Charlie had followed along behind her, but Vicky seemed to be ignoring her. Finally, she couldn't take the silence any longer. "Mom?"

"What is it, Charlie?" she said, without looking up.

"Are you upset?"

Vicky brought a knife down harder than necessary and sent a chunk of onion skittering across the counter and onto the floor. "Of course I'm upset. I barely saw you all day, and now you tell me you have to leave. I'm starting to wonder if I've overstayed my welcome."

It struck Charlie hard like a punch in the gut. "No! No, of course not! Mom, you know I want to spend as much time with you as I can. I've been having such a great time getting to know you it's just... there are other things I've got to do too."

"I just thought after almost twenty years apart you'd be able to put things aside for me. It's not like you have a nine-to-five job that you have to be at, or you'll get fired. You only work when you want to. So, you must want to." The tone was ice-cold, and Vicky still wasn't looking at her.

Charlie's stomach churned and she felt queasy. "It's not—that's not ... Sam needed me today. We both own the ranch, and he works every day so it's not really fair if I don't help out." It was the most vanilla explanation she could think of that might soothe her mother, but Vicky was having none of it.

"He's the foreman, you said. Seems to me like he should have things under control without needing my little girl to go pitch in." She sniffed derisively.

"He *does* have things under control, mom ..." She sighed. It was becoming clear that Vicky wasn't a big fan of Sam, and vice versa and she really hated to be between them. "Being in control means knowing when you need an extra pair of hands, and I'm not a little girl anymore. I'm a skilled worker who just happens to also own half of the ranch."

Vicky's mouth twisted unpleasantly at the latter part. "Half. I can't believe your father gave half of your inheritance away. I never would have expected Jimmy to be so cruel."

"Mom ..."

Charlie's attempt to explain the will again was interrupted when Vicky shook her head and then threw her arms around Charlie, hugging her tight. "You poor kid."

Charlie was getting used to her mother's sudden bursts of affection and relaxed into the hug. For so many years being hugged by Vicky was something she had only dreamed of, and it was nice to feel it for real. It just seemed like sometimes the older woman used affection to get in the last word, and then she'd feel guilty for suspecting her mother of ulterior motives.

In this case though it was just as well, and she let the defense of her father drop for the moment. She was still struggling with Jimmy's decisions too, so arguing in his favor wasn't exactly easy. Vicky's annoyance seemed to dissipate, as though she'd gotten it out of her system and finally things relaxed between them.

Charlie helped out in the kitchen, doing the actual cooking part as she stir-fried strips of chicken in olive oil. Vicky chopped vegetables and threw together the rest of the salad. It was fun working side-by-side in the kitchen. She enjoyed it and things seemed peaceful as they sat down to eat and chat.

But when her alarm went off and she explained that she had to go, it seemed to upset Vicky all over again. She didn't get angry, but her eyes filled with tears and her whole mood dropped leaving Charlie feeling guilty.

"I know we didn't get much time together today. I'm

sorry, but tomorrow I should be able to come over. Maybe we could go out for lunch. Around noon?" she suggested, hoping to raise her mother's spirits in the very limited time she had before she needed to dash.

"Sure. That sounds nice," Vicky replied. Her voice was almost monotone, and it was obvious she was still upset about it.

Charlie hesitated but the minutes were ticking away. "I'm sorry. I promised Sam I'd be home by seven, but we'll have tomorrow, okay?"

Vicky frowned and then shrugged. "I guess I don't have a choice. It's obvious the opinion of the foreman means more."

It hurt to hear that. Charlie felt her guts churning as the stress built. "Mom ..." She didn't know what to say. If she reminded her mother that Sam was also her boyfriend then her mother would complain about Sam controlling her—she'd implied that once already.

The older woman gave herself a visible shake and then held up her hand. "Don't try to convince me. It's fine. I can't expect to be the most important person in your life when I haven't even been around. I get it." She sounded so sad and empty.

Part of Charlie wanted to agree with her. There was still an undercurrent of resentment that her mother had walked out and never come back. She kept it pushed down because she didn't want to blame the woman for a decision that her father had made for both of them.

But another part of Charlie, the piece of her that desperately wanted this relationship to work, felt guilty. She blamed herself somehow for Vicky's sadness and it quickened a fear in her that it would chase Vicky away. Her mother, she could tell, wasn't someone who wanted to hang around being unhappy.

"It has nothing to do with any of that, but Sam goes to

bed really early and he wants to spend some time with me too—you get that right? I've been over here a lot since you arrived, and he just wants to see me before he goes to bed." It was the best she could do.

She put down the towel she'd been using to dry dishes as her mother rinsed them. She leaned in and kissed her mother lightly on the cheek. "Tomorrow we'll have a nice lunch out. It'll be fun!"

Vicky nodded, still looking upset, but she forced a smile and Charlie had to accept that because she was out of time. She offered a quick goodbye as she hurried out the door, and then jogged the whole way home. Luckily for her, she made it right on time because Sam was pointedly looking at the clock when she came inside.

"I'm here!"

"You are, barely. How was dinner with your mother?" He held out his arms and she ducked into them, melting against him with a happy sigh.

"Awkward and full of guilt for barely seeing her."

"Your guilt? Or your mother trying to make you feel guilty?"

She sighed. "A little of both I guess." More the latter but she wasn't going to get Sam started on her mother again. "Can we just cuddle and relax? I don't really want to talk about her."

He drew her over to the couch, where the fire was already crackling. He pulled her into his lap as he sat down, and they were quiet together for a few minutes. "I see you got the housework done, how about the school stuff?" he asked as she relaxed in his arms.

"I made a list of potential long-distance doctoral programs, and there's also one close enough that I could drive, so I'm considering that one too. As far as the pre-requisites I'm going to need a few things, but well … I admit I snuck in as many related classes as I could when I was going for my masters so it's not too bad. Maybe one semester worth before I can apply."

Sam chuckled. "I think I understood about half of that. I'll tell you a secret, little girl." He stared into the fire thoughtfully for a few moments as she waited. "When your dad sent you off to school, I was a little jealous. I always wanted to go on to college, but it just didn't work out that way."

It surprised her. Her mouth opened and then she snapped it shut as she thought about that. Sam had only been a teen himself when his father had died, and he'd stepped into a man's full-time work when it happened. It had never occurred to her that maybe he'd wanted something more than this.

It was funny really. Him wanting what she had, while she'd wanted nothing more than to stay on the ranch and run things with her father. She snuggled back into his arms and rested her head on his shoulder. "It's not too late, you know?"

"For what?"

"To go to school? If that's something you want to do there's no reason why you can't."

He laughed and shook his head. "Naw, darlin' that ship sailed a long time ago. What would I even do with a degree now?" He sounded amused and surprised by the suggestion, but she wasn't kidding.

"I'm serious, Sam. I mean, you're not just a ranch hand anymore. You're the foreman, and you're half owner of this spread. With so much being done online now you can have all the education you want."

He was silent and when she tipped her head back to look up at him, he seemed pensive. The firelight was reflected in his eyes, as he stared into it looking for answers. "I don't know. Doesn't seem much point now. And I'm pretty satisfied with my life. Not like I'm looking for a new career or anything. I just … there was more out there to know, and I was hungry for it."

That was the thing about Sam. He was smart as a whip. He downplayed it, and maybe in a way she'd overshadowed him when they were kids because of how she'd skipped grades, but she knew how smart he was. "You know … Daddy—" She reached up and ran her fingers along the line of his strong jaw, feeling the rough scruff of stubble. "you don't have to *do* anything with education. You can just have it, just to know things."

He looked down, eyebrows going up. "I guess that's true. I never really thought about it that way."

"Maybe if my father had just let me learn what I wanted I would have enjoyed college more. I hated being pushed away from the things I wanted to know, but you… you could study anything, just because you want to."

There was a lightening in his eyes, like a dawning sun and for a second she knew he was seeing all the possibilities, but then he shook his head. "Not saying I wouldn't enjoy it, but I don't know when I'd find the time."

"You can take one class at a time. Find the things you're interested in and we'll find a class for it online. We can study together. I mean, once I get into a doctoral program, I'll be studying a lot anyway. It might be more fun to do it together." And didn't it sound romantic in a weird way? At least it did to her.

He thought about it and after a long silence he nodded once. "I'm up for trying it out, but right now there's something else I want."

"What is it?"

"You. Yesterday was nice but not nearly enough to make up for all the time we've missed so I want you stripped and naked on the bed. Now." His voice had taken on the low husky sound that meant he had dark and delicious plans for them.

She wiggled, grinding down in his lap until he groaned and then she slid to her feet. She started stripping right on the spot and left a trail of clothes to the bedroom. He banked the fire, shut off the lights, and by the time he joined her she was sprawled on her back, posed artfully with one arm covering her breasts, and one knee up to hide the juncture between her thighs.

"Like what you see, Daddy?" She drew her tongue across her bottom lip slowly and watched as he undressed and dropped his clothes to the floor. He was a hardworking man with a lean muscled physique and seeing him like that made her want to lick every line, every muscle.

"Oh, yeah, but I think we need to get you some accessories." He opened a drawer and pulled out a coil of soft silk ropes. Just the sight of them in his hand made her wet. She let her thighs part, falling open to flash him the sight of her dark curls.

"Are you going to tie me up so I'm helpless to resist?" She felt a little thrill curling tight in the center of her body, a tickle that made her breathless.

He chuckled as he settled down on the bed, and it sounded like a threat of things to come. He grabbed her by the leg and hauled her over to him. "I think you're already helpless, baby. Don't you?"

"Mmmm, maybe. I could probably make it to the door if I put real effort into it." She eyed the dark doorway as if weighing her odds of success.

"Don't you dare, brat. I'm not chasing your ass, buck-naked in the cold and you wouldn't like what happened when I found you either." He growled and covered her with his body, nipping with sharp teeth at her shoulder. "Now be a good girl, so Daddy can tie you up."

She was ... fairly good. She couldn't resist struggling a little, that was part of the fun of being tied up to start with, but she only tried to make a break for it once. By then he'd already started wrapping the ropes, so it was a simple matter of using them as a leash to drag her back again.

He landed a hard slap on her left ass cheek, a reward for the playful attempt and she wiggled her butt until he gave her a second one on the right side.

"I guess someone has been running wild for too long. I'll have to take care of that." But there was no anger in his voice. This was all for fun and she was enjoying every second of the attention.

The punishment the day before had given her a brief escape from her own mind, blocking out all the stress and worry she'd been dealing with. That small window of quiet had made her realize how much she'd missed it when he took control, and she could just let go.

What her mother wanted didn't matter at the moment; even what *she* wanted took second place in those minutes. It was all about Sam and his control.

He trussed her up, wrapping the silken cords just tight enough to restrain as he arranged her body the way he wanted it. She ended up on her knees, spread wide, her arms were drawn under her body, between her legs and attached to her ankles. She rested on her shoulders with her head turned to the side. She watched as he patiently drew the ropes through, knotting them, testing how deeply they pressed into her flesh.

Her own arms kept her legs from closing, kept her glistening parts on display for him to feast on, but that wasn't enough for him. He wanted her even more bound. Ropes wound around her upper legs, just above the knee and then were dragged down on either side of the bed and tied to the frame.

He forced her knees farther apart by pulling and tugging the second leg until the stretch left her pussy lips gaping open and then he tied that one down too. There was something so vulnerable about that. An edge of embarrassment too, even though he was the only one who could see. The cool air tickled across the wet curls, and her clit tightened, demanding to be touched—but that wasn't up to her.

When he was done, all she could do was wiggle her fingers and toes. She might have been able to roll on her side if she was left alone long enough to get a rocking motion going, but that wouldn't happen. She was helpless, open for his touch or anything else he wanted to do to her.

It felt so freeing. The tension began to drain from her body, leaving her limp, and she let her eyes close to add to the anticipation. "I love this," she murmured.

"We haven't even gotten started yet, Charlie girl. Tonight might just be another short night for sleep." He sounded satisfied with his work, though he still plucked and adjusted ropes for a for another minute or so. He'd always been a perfectionist when it came to his bondage skills. She didn't care; she was content under his ministrations.

"I've got a surprise for you, baby. Want to guess what it is?" He'd leaned in close to whisper it in her ear.

"Is it … a spanking?"

She sounded so hopeful that he laughed. "That's not a surprise, that's a standard part of the package, and since I see all the welts are gone from my belt, I don't have to go easy on you." He stroked his rough, calloused hand across her ass, and she leaned into the caress.

"But no, I ordered a special surprise for you and it arrived today. Got any guesses?"

It could be nice, or it could be mean. With Sam there was just no way of knowing and the unknown filled her with nervous anticipation. "Is it a new spanking toy maybe?" she asked hesitantly.

"Good guess. Actually ... I did order a new implement too, but it's mean so I think I'll save it for punishing a bad girl. Any more guesses?"

The thought of a mean new toy shouldn't have made her gush, but it did. As far as ideas went though, she was tapped. It had to be specifically play-related but that could be almost anything. "No, Daddy. No more guesses."

"Well, then I guess you'll just have to wait and find out." He sat up, moving back on the bed and she took a deep breath, waiting for the games to begin.

CHAPTER 10

For a day that had started off having to punish Charlie, it had been a pretty good one. She hadn't put up a fuss when he'd given her chores to fill her day. Only the ranch work had technically been punishment. The rest was simply a matter of forcing her to catch up with things she'd neglected.

There *was* an ulterior motive there of wanting to limit her time with Vicky, and he intended to continue that. The way Charlie had meekly submitted to the list said a lot, and he had a feeling somewhere deep down she was grateful for an excuse to not be able to spend the whole day with her mother. He had every intention of keeping her on track and the fact that it would leave her less time was a bonus.

But a box he'd ordered a month back had arrived that afternoon and Charlie had been such a good girl in getting everything done that he'd decided to reward her *and* himself. He'd prepped everything before she'd come home and now he pulled out the box from under the bed.

"No peeking, Charliegirl," he warned her. She mumbled something vague in response but when he guided it between her thighs and gently rubbed it back and forth between her slick folds, she suddenly got a lot more interested.

"Oooh! What is that?"

"Still no guesses?" He laughed. "I would have thought you'd be able to tell."

"Is it a vibrator?"

It was, but not the usual dick-shaped one. This was a special toy, and he was hoping it lived up to its reputation because it hadn't been cheap. It was curved into a flattened U shape. The smaller part would slide inside of her while the larger bulb would rest directly against her clit. He couldn't wait to see her reaction.

"Very good. A remote-controlled vibrator to be specific." That was all the information he was going to give her. He turned it on at the lowest setting and then pressed one side down against her clit, just to give her a taste. It got an immediate reaction from her and he was amused at how she strained against the ropes trying to get more.

It didn't do any good, and he drew it away from the bundle of nerves to run it down between her soaked folds until it was covered in her juices. "I think you're going to like this. Now stay still like a good girl." He patted her ass in a light warning and then he slipped the smaller rounded end inside of her. It went into the slick passage easily and settled against her g-spot. Then he adjusted the other half to rest against her clit.

"Oh, that feels ... strange. That's different." She wiggled a little, probably trying to see if it would come loose, but the piece inside held the outer part firmly in place.

He turned it on to let her experience the full effect of the dual vibrations working together. The remote had plenty of options that would allow him to drive her crazy and he intended to go through all of them. "Ready to see what it feels like?"

"Yes!" She was obviously excited and raring to go, but the second he turned it on she began to strain and move. "It's— It's so... wow. I can barely think."

"And that's the lowest setting. Let's try something a little higher." He bumped it up a couple of notches. "And Charlie? You're allowed to come *once*, but after that there are penalties for any unauthorized orgasms. Got me?" He figured he had to give her that much. From everything he read it was going to be beyond intense.

She began mewling and moaning almost immediately which seemed to indicate that the hype wasn't faked. He sat back to watch her trembling as he changed the settings, going up and down as he listened to all the sounds she was making. Just listening to her had his cock hard and jutting straight up in the air.

He couldn't resist stroking himself slow and easy while he enjoyed the show, but it ended faster than he'd expected. One more notch on the remote and she shattered with a loud wail of pleasure. He turned it down a few levels, but not off.

"P-please Daddy, too much. T-too sensitive. Turn it off, please." The words were stammered and full of pleading as she rode out the orgasm and then immediately began to climb towards the next.

"It's a good thing you got home on time. I decided if you were late, I wasn't going to let you have this tonight." No harm in letting her know how close she'd come to missing out.

"I'm going to come, please. I c-can't stop!" The words were barely out of her mouth when they became true and she whined as a full-body shudder rolled through her.

"Uh-oh. I did warn you, Charlie." He tsked and made it sound like he was disappointed in her inability to hold back but he was actually pleased. Hell, he was getting more than he could have dreamed of. This toy was going to be perfect for rewards *and* punishment. "I'm going to have to punish you and then we'll try again."

He retrieved a thin plastic paddle from the drawer. It was little more than a child's toy but had a fierce sting. He didn't turn the vibrator off, but he did turn it down to the lowest setting. There was some curiosity about whether she'd be able to come even while he was spanking her, but mostly he just liked the idea of her fighting the opposing sensations.

With crisp burning slaps he peppered her ass with the paddle. The plastic was clear, so he got to enjoy the sight of her ass turning red as he delivered dozens of spanks. The ropes held her in place, giving her no escape from the sting, but the way her muscles tightened and her body twisted every time he snapped it down soon had another climax on the rise.

She began to push her backside back into the spanks, wanting them, wanting the orgasm that was so close to cresting, and right before she reached the edge, he hit the remote and the dual vibrations ceased. It took a few seconds for her to notice and then, "Daddddy nooo! I was so close! Please turn it back on!"

"Didn't you just ask me to turn it off a few minutes ago?" He let his amusement show and when she cursed him under her breath he laughed out loud. The paddle began to swing again, but now the fun part was gone leaving only the searing burn that had settled in and spread out across her entire ass.

He shifted his aim to her thighs and gave each one a couple dozen slaps to get the color rising there too. It was like a siren call to his hand and he couldn't resist setting the paddle aside so he could stroke and knead the burning flesh. He wasn't being gentle but the way she moaned and whimpered said she loved it.

Her inner thighs glistened with the proof of how much she was enjoying herself. "How many more do you need,

Charlie? What's fair for disobeying me and stealing an orgasm without permission? Another hundred?" he asked playfully.

She jerked and twisted around to make sure he saw the pout. "That's too many. I'll break."

"Will you?" He chuckled and shook his head. He knew her better than that. Not that he was actually intending to give her that many, but Charlie's pain tolerance was high. They weren't even close to her limits. "You could safeword. This isn't really punishment and you know that. Say red and I'll untie you."

They might not use safewords for punishment, but when they were playing for fun, he wanted them both to be enjoying the games. If she wasn't then he wanted to stop and see what was wrong.

But he knew damned well there was nothing wrong right now and that she had no intention of safewording. He ignored the glare she sent his way. "No? Guess we keep going then."

He picked up the paddle and began to smack it down in random spots, letting it be unpredictable, so she was never prepared. Some of them were hard, others were light slaps that would barely increase the growing sting. The crisp pop of paddle meeting flesh was loud in the cabin, and probably carried through the walls. But it sounded harder than it was, and he knew the effects were mostly surface level.

He could have continued all night; except he was starting to feel in need of some relief for his aching erection. It strained and bobbed and even the thought of being nestled inside her body made beads of pearly pre-cum appear at the slit. "You're so fucking beautiful," he said.

He set the paddle aside for the moment and pulled a bottle of lube out of the box. He'd known from the second he'd bought the vibrating toy that he wanted to take her ass while it she wore it. He wondered if he'd feel those vibrations too when he was settled deep in her back hole.

He slicked up his finger and pushed gently but insistently at the tight ring of muscle until she relaxed and accepted the intrusion. She was no longer new to anal play, and now tended to enjoy it, but there was always that initial bit of reluctance.

"Your other hole is filled, so I guess this one is for me, girl," he said, teasing her as he worked his finger in and out. He turned on the vibe, set to the lowest setting and that cleared up any more hesitation on her part. She rocked back on his finger taking him deeper.

There was a small gasp when he added a second and began to stretch, but she'd assured him she rarely felt any discomfort anymore, so he continued to widen her. Occasionally he paused to adjust the settings, turning them up or down as he played with her ass and prepared her for his cock. It didn't take long before she was begging for it.

"Please Daddy, please… I want you." Her voice was hoarse, rough with need and desire.

"You think you're ready for me, Charlie? You want me to take your ass?"

"Yes, yes please." That breathy way she had of begging made him want to shove into her with a brutal thrust, but he restrained himself.

"That's my good girl," he said, praising her as he pulled his fingers free with a lewd sucking sound. Her hole gaped wide, open and ready. He took just a few seconds to slip a condom on and slick himself up with lube before the head of his cock was nudging at her hole.

Despite the urge to thrust he held back, working his way inch by inch as she mewled and rocked under him. The feeling was indescribable. The tight constriction hugged his cock urging him further in and he groaned at how good it was.

He waited until he was almost fully seated before he reached for the remote. Without warning her he dialed it all the way up. She reacted with a gasp of surprise that turned into a long moan as she slammed back against him and took the final inch. He hadn't been able to feel much of the vibrator until then, but once he turned it all the way up, they both got a taste of the aggressive ripples as they transferred from her body to his.

It was a more intense experience all around. With the vibrator in her pussy, her back channel was even tighter, and now he could feel the waves of vibration stroking his cock through the thin wall that separated her holes. "Fucking incredible," he muttered, digging his fingers into her flesh as he held her in place. He pulled back with aching slowness and then snapped his hips forward.

His belly slapped against her sore ass, feeling the heat he'd raised with the paddle. He began to move, thrusting deep every time. He loved the feel of her spanked skin against him when he slammed home, especially since he knew that it would reignite that sting and set her to squirming against him.

It wouldn't last long. It couldn't; there was just too much sensation. The tightness of her back channel seemed to make every thrust more intense and he could already feel her body starting to shake as another orgasm built. When she climaxed and clamped down it was too much and pushed him into his own orgasm.

His balls tightened and pulled up warning him that he was about to hit his peak, and suddenly it was smashing over him like an avalanche. For a second he couldn't focus on anything but how it felt. Relief and indescribable physical sensations dragged all his attention to his cock nestled deep in her ass. He couldn't think beyond the physical as his body pulled him in two directions.

Trying to keep the pleasure going won, and his body shook with the effort to continue. The oversensitivity made it impossible to manage more than a couple thrusts and then he was done. Even slowly sliding out of her made him jerk and groan.

Charlie wasn't in much better shape. She twitched and whimpered but words seemed beyond her. She managed a few broken syllables that he understood to be begging, but it took him a second to fumble for the remote so he could shut the vibrator down. Actually, removing the device was beyond him at the moment, his hands were shaking too hard, and judging by the way she kept tensing and clenching around it, she was still dealing with aftershocks.

If the ropes hadn't held her in place, he had a feeling she would have collapsed by now. As it was, she somehow managed to look dazed even with her eyes shut. Her mouth gaped slightly, and her breath came in short pants punctuated by little sounds.

It had probably been one of the most intense sexual experiences of his life. Almost too much for him to want to try it again any time soon. He carefully shifted to sit on the edge of the bed, leaned down and managed to work the knot free holding her on that side. The other would have to wait until he wasn't shaking.

His hand settled lightly on her calf. "You okay, baby-girl?" His voice sounded harsh. He wondered if he'd shouted when he came. Honestly, he had no idea, but his mouth and throat were dry so that might be the cause, or a symptom.

"Mmmhmph." She didn't open her eyes, but she wiggled a little.

"I'll take that as a yes, I guess." He didn't have the energy to laugh and what he did have went into removing the vibrator and the ropes.

He'd planned ahead and used knots that could be untied with one tug in the right direction and he was grateful for that now. His hands were shaking too much to struggle with a stubborn knot. With one sharp pull on each line, they released, and he unwound them so he could check her wrists. Then he started working on her ankles.

It took her a minute to gather the energy, but finally she shifted and pulled her arms up in front of her so she could rest her head on them. Once the last of the ropes had slithered away, she tipped over on her side and just sprawled there.

She looked well-fucked and there was nothing more beautiful than knowing he'd put that wrecked look on her face. He wanted to crawl up beside her and crash, but he couldn't. Not until she was taken care of.

His body was reluctant to get up, but he managed. He stopped by the bathroom to dump the condom and clean up fast and then he went to the kitchen to get a glass of orange juice for her, and water for him. If she was as drained as he was, she'd need something.

She was asleep when he returned, and he had to nudge her awake and help her to sit up so she could drink some of the juice. He held the glass to her lips. "Big sips, baby. Judging by the wet spot on the bed you're about half dust right now."

She wrinkled her nose when she tasted the acidic bite of orange; it wasn't her favorite, but she obediently took a small sip. As though the liquid reminded her of how thirsty she was, she wrapped her hands around the glass and in under a minute had guzzled the whole thing.

"Want some more?" he asked as he set the empty on the nightstand.

She shook her head. "No, but can I have a sip of water to rinse the sweetness?"

He handed her his drink and didn't complain when she finished off half of it, but he did chuckle as she gave it back. He drained the rest and then settled her down on the dry side of the bed. He threw a towel over the damp patch and sighed. "You know, one of these days we're going to remember to put the towel down first."

But she didn't answer; she was already in dreamland. He barely had the energy to flop beside her, pull her into his arms, and then join her in an exhausted sleep until the alarm woke him up way too soon.

It had been worth it. Giving up sleep for that night had been an easy trade off to make and the extra tired was nothing that a long hot shower and a gallon of coffee couldn't fix. But if he'd known the shitstorm that was about to hit him, he might have chosen to get the sleep instead.

Okay, probably not, but it was a thought that popped into his head later.

He left her curled up asleep in the bed and went to work. He'd considered waking her up and dragging her along because if she was working on the ranch then she wasn't with Vicky, and that was a good thing. But she looked too peaceful there and he didn't have the heart to shake her awake.

Besides he didn't need her down there every day and she'd start to resent the time when she realized he was doing it to keep her out of her mother's clutches. He had to work something out, but that probably wasn't it. Later he'd question that choice too, but at the time it seemed right.

Sam was using one of the last good days to put some time into working with the black Devil horse. He had plans for putting him to stud but until he was tamed down a little that wasn't going to happen. The stallion had tried to savage the first mare that they'd put in with him, but he was making slow progress on getting the wild horse in line.

Today though, it just seemed like the stallion wasn't in the mood to behave and finally he gave up. He swept his hat off as he came out of the corral, wiping his forehead with a ragged, but clean-ish, bandana and leaned against the fence. "Damn horse," he muttered. Maybe it was time to turn him over to one of his hands. Most of them had a decent amount of experience and more time than he did.

"Hey, Sam? Got a minute?" It was Mike, with a look that practically screamed bad news.

Figures. "Yeah, what's up?"

"Well, uh, you know there's a moving truck up at the main house?" The hesitant way he said it made it clear that he didn't think Sam was aware.

"A … moving truck?"

"Yeah."

"Maybe they got lost? Took a wrong turn?" Sam sounded doubtful even to his own ears. They were way off the beaten track with a private road all the way back, and a big gate with a sign.

"Yeah, I don't think so. It's parked outside the house and things are being loaded onto it from the house. I didn't think much of it at first. I thought maybe Charlie was clearing out the clutter, but then I noticed she wasn't up there. Vicky is though." The last part was said in a different tone and it got Sam's attention.

Well, fuck. The last thing Sam wanted was a confrontation, but he needed to check it out. It's not like his mind jumped immediately to the idea that Vicky was robbing the house but … yeah, it was exactly that. "I'll go check it out," was all he said.

He strode up to the house double-time and sure enough he could see a steady progression of heavy old furniture being hauled out of the truck by several burly moving guys. He didn't stop to talk to them, but stormed into the house yelling, "Vicky! You here?"

He heard a faint response from the downstairs bedroom, Jimmy's old room, and he headed there. It was practically empty, and she was supervising the dismantling of the bed frame.

"Vicky, what's going on?" He tried not to sound confrontational, he really did.

He failed.

She gave him a surprised look and then one of her well-practiced smiles. "I would think it was obvious. I'm getting rid of this old junk furniture. It's much too heavy for the space, don't you think?" She sounded cheerful and he had to grit his teeth to avoid snapping at her.

"Charlie didn't mention she was clearing out this bedroom," he said. And he'd be having words with his little girl if she'd just forgotten to tell him something like that. She was allowed to do whatever she wanted with her furniture, but as her Daddy he wanted to know what decisions she was making. With something as potentially emotional as getting rid of her father's things he definitely needed a heads-up.

Vicky sniffed and her tone, when she replied, was icy. "I'm not sure why my daughter would need to inform a hired hand on *her* ranch that she was doing anything."

The snideness made his hands clench and he *really* wished he had the right to blister her ass because if he did his belt would have been off in a second. It wasn't often he longed for the good old days, but Charlie's mother brought that desire to dispense justice to the surface.

"Vi—"

"You may call me Ms. Townsend, if you don't mind. I prefer formality with the staff."

He stood there, staring at her in shock for a full minute

while he counted to ten backwards and forwards. When he could finally manage a response, his words were ice cold. "*Ms.* Townsend ... I'm sure you're aware that I'm not staff. I'm half-owner of this ranch and I'm your daughter's partner."

"You may have stolen half her inheritance, but you don't own *this* house, now do you? So, this is none of your business." She turned away from him and he reached out to grab her arm, then stopped before he touched her, turned on his heel, and stomped outside before he did something he'd regret.

The moving men stopped short and gave him a nervous side-eye. They could clearly see something was brewing and they didn't want to be involved in any of it, so they busied themselves inside the truck making sure things were packed safely.

Sam whipped out his cell and called Charlie. It took a while for her to answer, but she sounded awake enough when she spoke. "Charlie, quick question. Were you planning to do anything with the furniture in the big house? Your dad's bedroom set?"

"Uh ... I mean, I was thinking that after the remodel we might look at new furniture. The new brighter style isn't going to work with all the clunky old antique stuff, but I didn't have any plans to do it right now. Why?"

Sam took a deep breath and for a second he thought he'd save her the stress and leave her out of the loop. He wanted to protect her with every instinct in his body, but this ... this just wasn't something he could leave her in the dark on.

"Well, Vicky has a moving truck outside and she's emptying out the house. You might want to come up here."

Charlie gasped and then there was a silence. He was starting to think she'd hung up when she finally answered. "I'll be right there."

It took Charlie less than ten minutes to get there, but by then he'd already stopped the moving men and explained the situation. They didn't like the idea of being in the middle of a family matter, but they also didn't want to unload the truck again, not until they got paid anyway.

He waited outside so he didn't have to deal with Vicky. He was almost glad this had happened. This, at least, was something he could prove. She'd been caught red-handed and Charlie wouldn't be able to explain it away. It would mean the end of the stressful visit.

Or so he thought.

The upset expression Charlie wore when she jogged up made him want to pull her into his arms and hold her. But when he approached, she just shook her head and went inside. He followed her in because he wanted to back her up, but what he saw was a level of manipulation that he'd never seen outside of a made-for-tv movie, or maybe a politician's campaign speech.

"Vicky, what are you doing?" Charlie demanded. She crossed her arms over her chest and stared her mother down with glittering eyes. *That* was his fierce girl. The one who didn't take shit from anyone.

"Oh, there you are honey. I guess the surprise is ruined now ..." Vicky shot Sam a dirty look as though he'd caused the problem.

"What surprise? And why is my father's furniture in a truck?"

"Well, I—you're not upset, are you?" Vicky put on a concerned look that Sam was sure was completely fake. "I was just trying to help. You told me all about your new plans for the house and I knew this old stuff wasn't going to fit in, so I thought ... I thought how much fun it would be for us to shop for new furniture together. I got a price on this old stuff and set it up to go."

Sam was speechless and Charlie seemed uncertain. "I … you really shouldn't have done this without talking to me. I …" she trailed off.

Vicky's bottom lip quivered, and her eyes filled with tears. He had to bite down on his lip not to call her out on the blatant falseness, especially since Charlie seemed to be falling for it. "I'm sorry. I really didn't think you'd mind. I just … you've been so busy that I thought I would pitch in and help."

"Mom…"

"I mean I've been gone so many years. The least I can do is help you deal with this. I—I just knew how hard it would be for you to get rid of Jimmy's things. Grieving is hard and I wanted to save you from having to make the decision." She sniffed and delicately wiped at her eyes with one finger. "Did I do something wrong?"

Charlie looked like she was about to cry too, and Sam couldn't take it anymore. "Vicky these weren't your decisions to make. You had no right coming in here and moving things out. What the hell were you thinking?" he demanded.

He shook his head and continued before she could get a word in, "You're lucky I didn't call the cops when I saw the moving van up here. I thought someone was robbing the place—and maybe you were. This isn't cheap department store furniture. It's worth a lot and I'm sure you know that."

Vicky jerked, her eyes opened wide and both hands went up to her mouth like no one had ever spoken a harsh word to her in her life. She turned pleading eyes on her daughter. "Charlie are you going to let your boyfriend call me a thief?" Her voice was full of woe and tears and he knew it was bullshit.

But Charlie didn't. When she turned to him, he knew how this was going to play out. She had a placating expression as she reached out to settle her hand on his arm. "Sam, she was only trying to help. She's right. I mean— getting rid of his things would have been really hard."

"Of course, it's going to be hard, Charlie. But it's part of the grieving process and it's for *you* to decide when you're ready to let go, not her." He wanted to grab her and shake some sense into her, but instead he shoved his hands in his pockets forcefully.

"I—I know but, it was just a mistake. I'm sure she thought she was doing a kind thing for me." He looked in her eyes and saw that need to believe. She desperately wanted Vicky to be the mother she'd dreamed of and she was going to overlook almost anything that contradicted that picture.

"Charlie..." He didn't continue. What was he going to say? He could bring up the phone calls, but he had no proof it was Vicky. If he forced the issue, made Charlie choose between them, none of them would like the end result, he was sure of that much.

If Charlie did listen to him it would mean asking Vicky to leave and ending her childhood dream of having her mom back. If she sided with Vicky that meant she was disregarding him as her Dom and Daddy. It was an impossible choice for the already conflicted girl, and he wasn't going to do that to her.

He sighed and rubbed his temple with two fingers. *Fuck.* "Fine. It was a mistake, but now what are we going to do with the truck full of furniture? They aren't going to unload it again without being paid for the work."

Charlie bit down on her bottom lip and gnawed it as she considered. She seemed torn, and he couldn't blame her. "I guess, since it's already loaded ... I just—where is it going?"

Vicky, who had taken on a chastened sorrowful look, was quick to reply. "The antique store downtown. They love stuff like this. I'm sure someone will snap it up and be thrilled to have it—and *obviously* I wasn't going to keep the money," she added as she sent an accusing look in his direction.

Charlie sighed heavily. Her shoulders slumped and she seemed weary of the conversation. "Just let them take it. It would have to go anyway, and you can keep the money, Mom. I don't want it. You can use it for your new start."

Sam repressed the growl, holding it in. A muscle in his jaw jumped from the way he was gritting his teeth. He was sure Vicky had planned to keep the money all along, but that was something else Charlie wasn't ready to accept.

He knew he had to get out of there before he lost his temper. "Well," he said carefully. "it sounds like you have it all sorted out then. I'm going to get back to work." The sarcastic comment about being *just* a ranch hand he bit back. It would have hurt Charlie and Vicky wouldn't care.

Charlie said goodbye and kissed him on the cheek, but she was clearly distracted by the situation and he left her reluctantly. She was home and making dinner when he got off work that night, but things between them were strained. The meal was clearly a kind of peace offering but it felt like the peace she was brokering was between him and her mother.

She was quiet and only picked at her food listlessly until he put down his fork and sat back to address the issue. "You know we need to talk about this."

"It's really not a big deal, Sam." She didn't meet his eyes.

"It is a big deal, and you know it. She overstepped and it wasn't her place. You need to set up boundaries with her. We talked about this, Charlie." He was trying hard to keep his tone neutral, so he didn't upset her more, but he was frustrated, and it probably showed.

"She's my mother. She just wanted to make things easier for me."

"Charlie, you're an adult and she's a woman you haven't

seen since you were a kid. She can't just walk in and try to decide things like this. I'm your Dom, the man you willingly turned over control to, and even I wouldn't have jumped in and made that decision for you." His hand came down on the table hard and the dishes clattered as they jumped. Her flinch made him stop and take a deep breath.

She looked up. "Sam, that's different. I know you're right. Of course, I was mad too. It's just ... she's trying to build a relationship with me now, and she just went a little overboard trying to help. I talked to her and she won't do anything like that again," she assured him with all the earnestness of someone who was positive they were right.

He found himself giving ground again. Not because he didn't want to fight it, but because he knew that Charlie was being pushed into a painful place and he didn't want to make it harder for her.

She was his main concern. Everything he did was for her, but he had no experience in how to handle this. He probably should have pushed. Later he would regret it, but at the time he thought it was best to let it go.

"Okay, Charlie. As long as you're fine with it."

But the rest of the meal was silent and when they went to bed there seemed to be a distance between them that even the cuddling couldn't close. The next few weeks were the worst they'd had since they had come back together.

Charlie was careful to keep to her rules. She made an obvious effort to get her share of the work done and she didn't miss another shift at the ranch. He spanked her a few times, but the catharsis they both needed was lacking from the scenes. Even there the space between them was noticeable.

He found himself being reminded over and over about their first break-up and how strained and painful it had been in the weeks leading up to it. It had felt too similar to what was going on now, and that terrified him, but nothing he did seemed to help.

If he kept his mouth closed, he had to watch as Charlie sank further under her mother's influence. If he said something it seemed to push her away and she became convinced that he simply hated her mother and could only see wrong in her.

And maybe there was some truth to that. He did see motives in everything Vicky did, and maybe sometimes he overreacted about small harmless things, but he was pretty sure he was right about the woman. Underneath the sweet innocence there was something mercenary in her, and he had a feeling Charlie was just a means to an end. He couldn't figure out the goal, but he was sure there was one.

The final straw came unexpectedly during the workday. Charlie had ridden out to the winter pastures with a couple of men to check things over and he'd been in his office dealing with paperwork. When Mike stopped in to ask a question, he took the opportunity to talk to him about Vicky and what had been happening.

Unfortunately, he wasn't aware that Charlie had come back to grab something she'd forgotten. He didn't mean for her to overhear him telling Mike that he was sure Vicky had been the one calling around about selling the ranch, but that's exactly what happened. He just didn't find out until later.

When he got home that night, she'd left a note. It was short and he had to sit down as he read it through the second time.

Sam,

It's obvious you can't get over this dislike of my mom, and I get it. You want to protect me and that's what I asked for. But I heard what you said to Mike today, and I just feel like right now you're blaming her for everything that goes wrong.

She's planning to go in about two weeks, so I'm going to stay up at the big house with her until then. There will be less clashing that way and I can spend more time with her. I love you, but this has been really hard on me and I need some space for now. Please, don't be mad at me.

Love,

Charlie

After the third reading he crumpled the note and hurled it across the room. He was angry and frustrated. He wanted to storm up to the house, throw her over his shoulder and carry her home. He couldn't understand how she could be so blind to Vicky's true character and he felt like he was out of options.

He didn't like this, none of it. Charlie belonged at home with him and with her out of his sight how could he protect her? Was he even supposed to protect her now? What did needing space mean for their relationship? He certainly couldn't do much as her Daddy if she wasn't there.

Instinct told him that he needed to leave things alone and he cut short his desire to go and retrieve her. When he checked the bedroom, he saw that her drawers were empty … but her silly stuffed bunny was sitting comfortably in the middle of the bed. That was a good sign, he supposed.

That night sleep didn't come easily and when he finally did pass out the blaring of the alarm was painful. It felt like he'd barely gotten an hour before it went off. He was slightly embarrassed to find out he'd ended up cuddling her damn rabbit at some point during the night and tossed it aside with a snarl.

He decided right then and there that he wasn't going to put up with this for long. Space between them was the last thing their relationship needed. He tried to pull it together for work, but he found himself snapping and snarling all morning. The hands scattered, pretending to be busy every time he walked by, but he caught the curious looks that followed him.

They were wondering what was going on—well, so was he. Being a Dom didn't give him magic insight. He felt like he was supposed to fix things, and he had no clue where to even start. Everything was a mess, and he had no choice but to just sit there and wait for Charlie to make the next move.

He was a patient man but sitting around and waiting wasn't one of his strengths, so for both their sakes he hoped she figured out what was going on fast.

CHAPTER 11

She had nothing to complain about when it came to their sex life. Sam was an attentive lover who knew all her hot buttons and it was rare that she didn't hit climax when they made love—unless he purposely kept her from it, of course. That was hot on a different level and the frustration of not being allowed to come eventually made it all worth it so she couldn't even hate it as a punishment.

And they'd played with sex toys before. In their arsenal were several including an egg and a vibrating butterfly that strapped on. They always added to the fun and the mystery surprise had gotten her all excited wondering what he had planned. Not that she'd needed much to get there when he started wrapping the ropes around her body. The helplessness of being tied was a big turn on, but she hadn't expected the dual vibes buzzing against her clit and g-spot at the same time.

She wasn't just wet, she was soaked. Her juices flowed like a river down her inner thighs. She'd never felt anything so deliciously overwhelming in her life. And then he started playing with her back hole, opening it with his fingers, she realized they'd only just gotten started.

He worked his thick erection in, and it seemed tighter than usual. The stretch from the double penetration erased any concentration she had left. It was just on the edge of being painful until she got used to the feeling of being stuffed.

She couldn't think, all she could do was feel the waves that were rolling through her body. He'd taken it slower than usual, but she was fine with that because she wasn't sure she could have handled any fast thrusting.

But when he began to move, she discovered that filling her back passage had pushed the vibrator even tighter against her g-spot. Every time he moved, it caused a ripple of pure pleasure that had her crying out and making barely human sounds.

By the time he was done, every muscle in her body was shaking and she was begging him to shut the toy off, because she was positive she'd die if she came one more time. She felt raw, fucked to the point of exhaustion and only the ropes held her upright. As soon as they came off, she just collapsed on the spot, whimpering.

She was drooling, and not just from her mouth. Normally she'd be trying to get to the bathroom to clean up before the sheets got soaked but she didn't have the energy to bother. Wrecked. That was the word for it. She was absolutely wrecked with pleasure.

It was no wonder that she didn't wake up when Sam left, or that she climbed out of bed much later than usual. The only thing that surprised her was that he'd been able to get out of bed and go to work. She remembered the way he had shouted and shook when he'd finally shattered inside of her, so she wasn't the only one who'd had an amazing experience.

It was going on ten when she crawled out of the warm

covers and hit the shower. She was stiff, sore in various places both inside and out, so she made it a long one. Plans for the day hadn't yet become a priority when she heard her phone. It took her a few minutes to find it in the pile of discarded clothes on the floor in the living room.

When she saw it was Sam she started to smile, but that smile vanished almost immediately when he informed her that there was a moving truck up at the big house and it was being loaded with furniture. For a second she wondered if they were being robbed and then her mind skipped over to Vicky.

She knew, without a doubt, this had something to do with her mother. She worked herself up into a furious tirade as she finished getting dressed and ran over to confront Vicky. She was *absolutely* furious. She really was, but then ... somehow her mother turned it all around.

Again.

Charlie didn't really understand how that kept happening with Vicky. Somehow the woman always seemed able to change things on her. Every time she got mad her mother had some excuse that seemed reasonable. And even when she wanted to stay mad, somehow she couldn't.

Charlie felt unprepared to deal with any of this right now. She'd gone from sleeping off a night of amazing sex to ... she wasn't even sure what was happening anymore. Part of her didn't know what to do. She felt like she was being torn in two directions and no matter what choice she made someone was going to be mad at her.

Vicky acted like she was sincerely sorry, and her explana-tion made sense in a way. At least, Charlie could twist her point of view around to seeing her mother's side. At the same time, she got why Sam was pissed. Underneath it all she could still feel a low grumble of anger too.

It had just been spackled over with the need to soothe

things between Sam and her mother because she couldn't deal with them fighting. Letting Vicky have the money from the furniture didn't help and she knew it, but she honestly didn't want it. In a way it would feel like she was selling her father's memories. Better to let her mother keep it, she thought.

Sam hadn't been pleased about it, but she hadn't thought about that before she'd said it impulsively, so she'd deal with it later. He left and she could tell he was struggling to keep control, so she let him walk out because it was one less person to focus on.

The tightness in her chest and her racing heart were enough to deal with. It was a struggle to push away the panic attack that tried to overwhelm her. Exercises were only going to go so far if things like this kept popping up at her unexpectedly.

She took a ragged breath and let it out. "Please don't do anything like this again, Mom."

"I was only trying to help, honey." Vicky sniffed and then dabbed at her eyes again. "I didn't mean to cause so much trouble."

"I know. It's— I understand, but please, don't do it again. I'm glad you're here but these are my decisions to make." Charlie sighed and rubbed her forehead as she looked around the nearly empty room. There was a line of boxes by the wall and she went over to look inside. Her father's clothes, all neatly folded, filled them.

"You're right. I guess I have to accept that you're an adult now. I suppose I can't really protect you from the hard things. I missed my chance for that when you were younger, and we can't turn back the clock. My fault..." There was a soft sound, like a muffled sob and Charlie knew without looking that Vicky was crying.

A mean thought rushed through her mind that if Vicky

really wanted to help, she'd be the one comforting Charlie instead of the other way around. She felt a stab of guilt for thinking it. She pushed aside her own upset to pull her mother into a hug. "You can't make decisions for me, but I appreciate you trying to help. I do."

Vicky clung to her. "I don't think your boyfriend likes me much at all... I don't understand why; he barely knows me. He accused me of terrible things before you got here. I think —maybe I should just go. I would hate to cause trouble between the two of you."

Charlie stiffened and pulled back. That was exactly what she was afraid of, but she tried to stay calm. "Don't be silly, Mom. You can stay as long as you want. Sam's just ... he's protective of me. He always has been since we were kids."

"But I really think he wants me to leave. I know I interrupted your plans on the house and I—"

"It's *fine*. The construction will happen, and Sam will relax when he gets to know you." Charlie somehow doubted that, but it would be nice if it did happen.

The look on Vicky's face said she didn't believe that either. Her pretty mouth turned into a frown. "I don't know..."

Charlie could feel her stress levels rising. The thought of losing her mother now was enough to make her stomach churn. "Mom, promise you won't vanish on me. Not after we're finally getting a chance to know each other."

"I—"

"Please?" Charlie poured everything into that plea. All her emotions and the need for Vicky to stay echoed in the single word, and she watched the older woman's waffling expression resolve into a slight smile.

"If that's what you want, honey. I guess I can stay a little longer." She sniffed and shook her head. "Not like I have any place to go yet anyway. I'm still working on a few things, but in two weeks I should have a place."

"Well, until you do, you can stay here," Charlie said firmly.

Vicky acquiesced, and Charlie okayed the moving van's departure. It felt weird saying goodbye to the heavy old furniture that had been in the house longer than she had. In a way it was like saying goodbye to her father again and she turned away long before the truck was out of sight.

She spent the early afternoon with Vicky and neither of them brought up what had happened. Her mother didn't even complain when she left before sunset, and Charlie appreciated that because she wanted to get home before Sam. Having dinner ready on the table would probably help to calm him down.

She had no doubt he was still going to be mad about what happened, and she was right. Dinner was strained as they both ate in silence. She kept thinking about what Vicky had said and wondered if Sam had really accused her of something. Had he been rude to her mother? Or was Vicky just overreacting from upset, as she was prone to doing.

She'd hoped being home when he arrived, with dinner ready, would soothe the problems so they could just move on, but it didn't work. Talking about it didn't help either and she kept thinking about what Vicky had said. She was starting to feel like maybe Sam did have issues with Vicky that he couldn't look past. It was painful and she didn't know what to do.

Over the next few weeks Vicky behaved like the perfect mom. She went out of her way to plan fun things for them to do together, even things that obviously weren't her cup of tea. A disastrous attempt at baking cookies together had them both waving the smoke out the back door and laughing. But despite the failure to create snacks, Charlie felt closer than ever to her mother.

Vicky even seemed to be making an effort about Sam. She stopped sneaking in underhanded criticisms and even asked how he was.

Sam on the other hand ... well, he didn't bring up Vicky but the stern worried look on his face all the time was probably related. Anytime she mentioned her mother it made him twitch and his answers were always careful and neutral.

She appreciated not having to fight about it, but what she wanted was for Vicky and Sam to be friends, if not family. And she couldn't help but see Sam's stubbornness as the barrier to that happening, because Vicky was at least willing to pretend.

Sam wasn't really the problem in this situation, and she knew it. She just couldn't admit it because then she'd have to explain that she wanted Vicky there enough to overlook the problems. She wasn't stupid and she had occasional moments of clarity about who was causing the trouble, but they were fleeting and vanished when she spent time with her mother.

She was sure eventually things would get better, but then it all came crashing down. She'd been picking up at least two days a week at the ranch and that morning she'd ridden out to the winter pastures with a few of the hands, just to check on things.

The herds had shelter and water, and there was no snow yet so they would still be able to forage for food. But if the grazing was getting lean, they'd need to cut open bales to add to the feed. Halfway there the hands split up and headed off in different directions. That's when she realized she'd forgotten her pocketknife on Sam's desk. It was a dumbass mistake and she cursed herself as she turned the horse around and headed back to the main barn to snag it.

But just outside of Sam's office she heard her name mentioned, and then Vicky's. Naturally she stopped to listen. Sam sounded so angry, so cold as the two men talked. His theory that Vicky had been the one calling around about selling the ranch came out.

Charlie covered her mouth to muffle the gasp. She couldn't really even process that possibility at first. The idea that Vicky would step that far over the line hit her hard, but Sam believing that and not telling her was just as painful.

She couldn't handle confronting him about it, especially not with Mike there in full agreement that Vicky was a horrible person. She backed out of the barn feeling numb and was faced with the waiting horse. As much as she wanted to run away, she still had a job to do.

With a borrowed knife she headed back out to the field. She went through the mental checklist without conscious thought, barely paying attention to the cattle that crowded around her to get at the hay she released. Once she was done, she took care of her horse and then went home.

She waited for the expected panic attack, but it didn't come. Instead, there was just a complete lack of emotion as she sat at the kitchen table lost in thought. She felt detached from her body, but not in a good way. It wasn't the fun floating separation that came from a good scene. This was a cold emptiness.

She replayed the conversation. Was Sam right? Had Vicky been the one looking for interested buyers? She couldn't fathom the motivation. It wasn't like her mother had legal rights to the ranch, so she couldn't have made any decisions no matter who was interested.

Plus, with the will in place the ranch couldn't really be sold at all unless they got permission from the lawyer who controlled the estate. Charlie couldn't have sold it even if she wanted to, so what would have been the point. Only...

It did occur to her that Vicky hadn't known that at the time. She clearly remembered the conversation about Sam being half owner had come up *after* those calls. Her fingers tapped restlessly on the table as she carefully pulled it all apart.

Sam could be right. It actually made sense in a way. Vicky hated the ranch and had done her best to wean Charlie off the work. There'd been talk about traveling together. Vicky had outright suggested that if Charlie sold it off, she'd be free to do more with her life.

Charlie had edged out of the conversation and it hadn't come up again, but she knew how her mother felt. Selling it off would please Vicky, but even before she'd found out that Sam owned half, she must have known she didn't have any authority to make those decisions.

Unless … Charlie thought about her father's furniture and the way Vicky had arranged its sale without even asking. Had she thought she could do that with the property? Unlikely, even the most naïve person had to know you couldn't sell someone else's property, but maybe she'd been trying to *help* again.

She'd wanted to save Charlie the trouble of dealing with her dad's furniture. Maybe she'd wanted to set things up for the property so that she could present Charlie with a finished deal. Charlie drew in a shuddering breath and let it out in a sharp laugh.

Helping. Vicky's idea of help was turning out to be the opposite, but she could kind of see the reasoning. It was wrong, obviously, but if she'd convinced herself she was *helping* it did make sense.

It also explained why Sam had been so angry at Vicky, so convinced she was a terrible person. Her poor Daddy was trying to protect her. He just didn't understand Vicky's motives. And no matter what she said he wasn't going to understand because his defensive mode had been activated.

She loved that protective Daddy side of him. She was his girl and he wanted to keep her safe from the world, but this time that wasn't going to work. It wasn't the world causing problems; it was her mother, which planted her directly in the middle.

They'd have a giant fight, and it would be painful for both of them. In the meantime, Vicky wasn't going to be there that much longer, and she didn't want the last of their time to be ruined with spillover stress. Especially since her mother had already promised not to do anything else like that.

Really the situation had already been dealt with so there was no reason to let it explode again, but she knew Sam wasn't going to accept that. Packing her things and leaving a note for him was the only thing she could think of that would keep things from spiraling. She'd just spend Vicky's last two weeks with her up at the big house. After she was gone Charlie would come home, and everything would be perfect again.

It should have worked like that. She wanted it to. But she should have known better.

Sam gave her three days before he came up to the big house and she knew he had every intention of dragging her home. She could see it in the flinty stare and the tense lines of his body. And she wanted to go with him so bad it hurt.

Three days of non-stop Vicky was wearing her down. Vicky continued to maintain that she'd be leaving in a couple of weeks, but she had plans for them to visit each other. She talked about the trips they'd take together. She wanted Charlie to spend the summer with her.

It all sounded very nice, but not really possible. She had the ranch and plans for school that weren't going to make it easy to do all the things Vicky wanted. Not to mention Sam would definitely have an issue with it. But when she tried, gently, to explain this to Vicky, she just didn't seem to ... take it in.

She started to worry that Vicky wasn't going to accept things not going her way, and when she realized that all her plans weren't going to happen ... Charlie didn't know how that was going to go. She'd already been worried that once Vicky left that would be the end of their contact. After all, that's what had happened when she was a kid.

But if Vicky was upset that Charlie didn't give her everything she wanted, it made it even more likely that she'd vanish. It became even more important that she spend every minute she could with her mother before she left, just in case.

"I can't, Sam."

"Why? Charlie, damn it, I don't like this. We were supposed to be beyond this back-and-forth crap. You promised no more running away. That's why you moved in, remember?"

"I know. It's just ..."

"If you heard me talking then you know what I suspect. You can't tell me you didn't consider the possibility that it was true when you heard me say it."

"I did, and maybe you're right, but it doesn't matter. It was –she was probably just trying to help, and she won't do it again. I talked to her after the furniture so it's not really an issue."

"Not. An. Issue?" He stared at her with incredulity written all over his face. "Are you kidding me? Of course it's an issue!"

She sighed. "I admit if she was the one who did that it's ... bad. But it's like with the furniture, she wanted to make things easier for me. It was wrong but it's over and I just want to let it go."

"You …" He swept his hand down over his face like he was trying to wipe the stress away. "I want you home. Now."

She shifted from one foot to the other, feeling trapped and unsure what to do. Fighting with him was hard enough, but she was also fighting with herself. Whatever she might have decided was moot because the next thing she knew Vicky had stormed out of the house looking like she was ready for battle.

Sam and her mother squared off for an epic fight and Charlie just wanted to vanish. The two of them hurled barbed insults and accusations back and forth. Neither noticed that she'd slipped into the house and gone to hide in her childhood bedroom, where she'd been staying for the past few days.

She needed something to keep her hands busy and she still hadn't unpacked her clothes, so she upended her bag on the bed and began to tuck them away into the dresser drawers. It didn't matter if she was staying or going, she just needed something to do to keep her mind off the fighting.

At the bottom of the bag, she found a surprise. She'd been in a hurry to pack and get out of the house before Sam could come home and talk her out of things, so she hadn't noticed when she'd scooped up her dad's letter with her clothes. Still unopened. Still a mystery.

She'd never entirely forgotten it existed, but it was easy not to think about it while it was nestled out of sight at the bottom of a drawer. Maybe now it was time to finally see what he had to say. She still didn't feel emotionally prepared for it, but then maybe she never would.

She curled up on the bed and stared at the creased and worn envelope. It had sat there for so long, as she'd put off reading her father's last words. It felt like an ending of sorts. As long as the envelope was sealed and she didn't read it, then he wasn't truly gone.

But it was time, past time maybe. She took a deep breath and carefully ripped along the seam. There was another hesitation before she unfolded the papers inside, but just a brief one. She was as ready as she was going to get.

It would be funny, she thought, if after all the buildup and long wait the letter was just some laundry list of details he wanted her to know. Maybe it would just be passwords and pin numbers. She doubted it; it was far too thick. But wouldn't she feel stupid for putting it off if that's all it was?

She laughed and unfolded the letter to find four pages covered with her father's familiar handwriting. But the smile quickly dropped from her face as she began to read.

Hey there, Charlie girl,

If you're reading this then I guess I've ridden off into the sunset and I bet you're pretty mad at me. I can't say I blame you. Some of the decisions I made must have seemed unfair to you at the time and looking at it now, I guess they were.

I had my reasons, if it helps any. Probably doesn't, but maybe this letter will clear everything up. I feel like a man's last words should be something special, but I'm not the best with things like that, so forgive me if I don't wax poetical.

These are things I wanted to tell you in person, but I never got the chance. Towards the end I—well, I'm ashamed to admit that by then I was scared. I didn't want to leave this world with my only daughter hating me. Selfish, I know, but there were a lot of things I never told you.

There was always a reason. You were too young. You were struggling to deal with things. You needed to mature a little more. And then things were so strained between us, and I was dying. It never seemed like a good time, I guess. So, this is my last chance to fill you in on all the things I should have told you.

First off, you need to know that I love you more than anything in this world or the next, kiddo. You're my pride and joy and I know you are damn capable of anything you put your mind to. My reasons for what I did, well they had nothing to do with not believing in you. I hope you'll realize that by the end of this.

This is hard so I'm just going to say it. I lied to you about your mom, or at least I didn't tell you everything and that's on me. Now that I'm gone, I can't hide this from you anymore. You need to know because I'm pretty sure you're going to have to deal with her before long.

I met Vicky in Vegas. My dad was still running things here and I took some time to sow my wild oats, I guess you could say. I knew I'd return to the ranch eventually, but I wanted to see a bit of the world before I settled down. There was a lot of drinking, a lot of gambling, and I was always good at those two things. I made a stack of money.

Looked up from a pile of chips to see this gorgeous creature smiling at me, and next thing I knew we were married. I'm not saying I was too drunk to know what I was doing. There was no surprise waking up to find out I had a wife. Nothing like that.

She was beautiful, clever and fun to be with. I wanted her and it became pretty clear she wanted me. Or so I thought. It was a mistake all around. Vicky wanted the fancy big spender she thought I was when I was riding high at the craps table.

She liked Vegas and I was having a blast, so we got an apartment and lived it up for a while. Neither of us really knew each other well, but we had fun until I got the call that my father had died, and I needed to come home and take over. That's when I got the first hints that there were going to be problems.

I showed up home with my new wife and let's just say it

didn't go well. I think she was expecting a rich man hobby ranch, something fancy. She hated this place from the moment she set foot on the property. I think she decided right then she was going to talk me into moving to the city, but I was in love, and when it came to her, I had a blind spot.

By the time I realized that she wasn't who I thought she was, you were on the way and I was stuck. No regrets on that score though. I wanted you from the moment she told me she was pregnant, Charlie. Whatever I feel about your mother, she did give me you.

I could go into detail of the many schemes she tried, but there were too many to count and I don't think you need to hear all of that. Once she realized that I was never going to walk away she stopped trying to talk me into selling it off so we could move and started sabotaging things.

She tried to get my best men fired. She turned them against me, spreading rumors that I was closing up and selling everything off. When they started quitting, I didn't put it together at first. I should have known by the fact that she'd seemed to finally settle down and accept the life. I wanted to think she'd found some contentment in it, or at least in me and you.

She was so good at telling me what I needed to hear. Sometimes she knew what that was even when I didn't. It's a gift I'm still in awe of and it allowed her to manipulate me six ways from Sunday. It was uncanny and I'm usually a good judge of character.

I'm ashamed of how long it took me to figure things out and of what happened next. See, I'd given her a bargaining chip. If there was one thing I loved more than the ranch it was my daughter. You. So, she threatened to leave and take you with her.

She said she'd take you somewhere I'd never see you again. Back then courts tended to favor the mother. I thought I'd win but I couldn't be sure, not really. And Vicky was so good at manipulating people. So good at crying until she got what she wanted.

Charlie set the letter down with shaking hands, unable to go on to the next page yet. Her heart was thudding hard in her chest and she'd gone cold. She didn't want to continue to read it. Whatever was coming next wasn't going to be pleasant. She knew that for sure.

It was already pretty bad. She couldn't help comparing her experiences with Vicky to what her father had dealt with. She always went into a conversation with her mother determined to set firm boundaries. Yet every time she somehow got turned around and ended up agreeing to things she didn't want.

She could never quite figure out how it happened. As Jimmy had said ... it was uncanny. The manipulation, she'd seen that too. And suddenly all those subtle comments about Sam and how he was just a ranch hand made sense. Vicky had been working to undermine her relationship with Sam from the start.

Why hadn't she seen that? Over and over, she'd dismissed Vicky's behavior as a mistake, or well-intentioned. "She was just trying to help," that was what she'd said to Sam.

Distantly she heard shouting, and then a door slamming. She registered it, but she wasn't able to process any new information at the moment. Her mind was swirling with too many thoughts and emotions. She blinked back tears repeatedly, but finally just let them fall.

She cried for the mother she'd always dreamed of. A woman who apparently had never existed. She cried for the relationship she'd tried so hard to build, tainted now by the truth she found in her father's letter. There were a few tears just for the stupidity of falling for it again and again, even while Sam had tried to warn her.

Her face was itchy with salt by the time she was done, and she was distracted by the sound of a truck roaring by the house at full speed, scattering gravel. With a dim kind of awareness she thought, *that's Sam.*

But she was determined to finish the letter. Whatever horrible stuff filled the final two pages she was going to push through it. She'd made a mistake by not reading it earlier, but it wasn't too late. She forced herself through a series of breathing exercises, drawing them out until her chest loosened.

There was no way she was going to relax with half the letter still unread, but at least the panic had retreated. She sighed and flipped to the third page.

She threatened to take you with her and go. I was scared for you. She had no life skills, not even a high school diploma. Though you wouldn't know it from talking to her. She was smart, maybe as smart as you are, Charlie.

She'd never really had to look out for herself and I knew if she took you and left neither of you would do well. Plenty of strong women get by on their own; Vicky isn't one of those. She told me once that she was pretty enough not to worry about how to pay the bills. I guess she was right.

I was upset at the thought of losing you. Couldn't have cared less if she left at that point, but I didn't want her taking you. Of course, she knew that. She knew before she made the threat that I'd do almost anything to keep you home with me. So, she waited for the right moment and then pulled the trump card.

She made me an offer I couldn't refuse, and I took it.

I'd get custody of you and in exchange I'd pay for her to

go live her life however she wanted. She set the terms, giving herself a pretty hefty chunk of money, which I was to deposit in her account monthly. We negotiated on the sum, but she knew she'd get most of what she wanted.

But to my shame I added my own conditions, and I'm sorry that I never thought about how it would affect you. I still don't know if I was wrong, but my part of the agreement was that she could never see you again. No phone calls. No letters. Nothing, or else I'd cut off the payments and we'd fight it out in court.

Vicky agreed, like I knew she would, and she left. We were always in touch, of course, had to send that money her way. She insisted that you get an education. Didn't want me to hold you back on the ranch, which she never thought was suitable for a girl anyway.

I agreed to make sure you got a proper education, so you could decide what you wanted to do with your life. I gave her my word on that, but to be honest, I agreed with her there. Part of me always thought that if Vicky had gotten an education, a way to channel all those smarts of hers, maybe she'd have turned out different.

Her parents didn't think a girl needed an education. They sent her brother instead and she left home angry about it, without even finishing high school. I think it warped how she saw the world, and I wanted it to be different for you.

I think your mother loves you, in her own way. She knew I'd do right by you, and she made me promise to give you what she never got, knowing I always keep my word. I just think that Vicky's first priority has always been Vicky. But that kind of influence isn't healthy for a kid. I wanted you to grow up better than she did.

So, I made sure you got the best I could give you. You got everything you needed, but you learned about hard work too. I made sure you saw and experienced more than just this rough old spread, even though you fought me at every turn.

You only wanted the ranch, and I was so proud of that. You're so damn much like me, Charlie. I hated sending you off to school, but that was the deal.

I know I messed some things up and I'm sorry for that too, but I tried, Charlie. I honestly tried my best. I guess ... I thought you'd be better off without her in your life. You were so young then too, maybe you'd forget if we never talked about her. So, I cut the memory of her out of the house, or I tried to, and I did my best to raise you on my own.

We did okay, I thought, but then I went and got cancer and that threw a wrench in the works. Didn't see that one coming. All I could do was try to tie up the loose ends before I was gone and that included seeing you through your education. I knew you'd quit if I wasn't there.

It also didn't escape my notice that cutting your mother out of your life made you slow to trust and commit to people. I've watched you push people away out of fear, and I have to take the blame for that. But Sam always seemed immune. It's one of the things I liked about him. He didn't give up on you, even when you struggled.

Yes, of course I knew you and Sam had a thing going. Neither of you were any good at secrets. It was obvious how much you loved each other. Hell, his dad and I used to talk about how one day you kids would probably get married. It got so I had to make extra noise if I checked the barn at night, just in case the two of you were in there messing around.

Sending you off to school while Sam stayed to take care of things for me caused more damage than I expected, and I regret that. I wish there'd been another way.

I've tried to fix things by throwing you together with the will, and that might have been a mistake. Only time will tell, I suppose. I'm guessing you're mad about it. I probably would be too if my meddling old man tried to play matchmaker with my inheritance, but there's a couple things here.

Firstly, I feel responsible for the distance between you two and I wanted to see if I could give you a shot at repairing it. But second, family ain't always about blood, Charlie girl. Sam might not have my genes, but he grew up here and I feel like he's part of the family. That and he went above and beyond what I expect from a ranch hand or a foreman.

You aren't going to be here for the end, not if I can help it. No child should see their parent like this. But Sam's going to help me through until it's over. He takes care of the ranch during the day and then sleeps on the couch over here to make sure I'm okay all night.

He's changed more piss soaked sheets than I want to think about, and held me while I puke from the morphine they've got me on to keep the pain down. When I wrote the will, I didn't know how bad things were going to get. But since then, he's earned a share of this place for that alone.

So, maybe you'll remember that you two love each other and run the place together as a couple. That's what I'm hoping for, but if not, I've made sure you're both taken care of and that's what I needed to do. Try not to be too mad that I split it between you.

I know you expected to run the place when I was gone, but it's good to have a partner in this life. Ranching can be exhausting, lonely work. This way you'll both have each other to shoulder the load. Whether you find that love you lost or not, I hope you'll at least become friends again, the way you always were before.

I really struggled with the decision to put him in charge of things instead of making you equals from the start, and I'm sure that had you ready to chew nails. But I know you, stubborn daughter. Without someone on top to make the decisions it would have been constant fighting between you. Since he's been running the place pretty much by himself since I got sick, I figured the boss should be him.

But people learn and grow. Figured it would be fair to give you a chance to get an equal say later, once you had time to be part of running things for a while. Experience is everything in this business, so I'm giving you a goal and I'm making it mandatory, so I can rest knowing I kept my word.

Finish your education, and by then I'm sure you'll have a better idea of all the work that goes on behind the scenes. Sam's not the type to keep you in the dark. Learn from him. Listen to him. Then when you've got your degree, you can sort out between you who'll be the boss. Or just leave things the way they are. That's up to you.

If you do decide to sit on your stubbornness and let the ranch go to him in seven years, then I've made sure you've got more than enough money to buy half back from him. The way that boy looks at you like you hung the moon and stars I have no doubt he'll let you, so either way you'll end up in the same place.

I'm leaving you all the options I can; only you can decide what you do with them. I love you Charlie. You made me proud every day of your life.

Your dad,

Jimmy

P.S. I kept paying Vicky long after you hit eighteen, just to keep her out of the picture. As long as she gets her money, she's been content to stay gone, but I deliberately made no arrangements to continue after my death.

She'll be notified by the lawyer as soon as it happens, so I expect it won't be long before she comes around to see what she can get. You need to be prepared. I know it's not going to be easy but try not to let her get the best of you, sweetheart.

She dropped the last page, letting it fall to her lap. For a while she just stared off into the distance. She wasn't really even thinking about what she'd just read at first. It took time to work through the sheer avalanche of emotions the words had inspired.

Her father's last words. She wished she had Sam there, holding her in his strong arms. It would have made it easier to face this final goodbye. It was going to take a lot of time to process everything he'd said. There was so much ... so much she'd misunderstood, gotten wrong.

If she'd just opened the letter that first day ... most of her anger and frustration would have dissipated. She couldn't argue with his reasons, not now that she knew the whole story behind them. And sharing with Sam hadn't turned out so bad.

There were many things about running a ranch that she had never seen when her dad was in charge. He'd taken care of all of it and everything she knew was just the physical side of things. She'd slowly learned through Sam that there was so much more to it and she was content now for him to be in charge. For now.

When it came to the stuff about her mother, well, that was harder to accept. The warm, loving woman she'd come to know didn't seem anything like the woman her father had described. And yet—and yet, so many times she'd found herself agreeing to things just to make Vicky happy.

She wanted to hold onto the hope that maybe Vicky had changed over the years. People did grow up, maybe her mother had, but she was full of doubt now. If she'd opened the letter earlier and gone into the relationship with those doubts in place maybe she would never have given Vicky a chance at all, but now she was knee deep in a complicated mess.

She folded the letter carefully and tucked it into the undersized pocket of her skirt. She'd show Sam and they'd talk it over together before making a decision. He was her Daddy after all. It was his job to help her with the hard choices and back her up while she made them.

It was only then that she remembered hearing a truck go by and wondered if he'd gone somewhere. It was quiet in the house, so the argument was over at least. She'd go see what was going on.

Halfway down the stairs she heard her mother talking in low tones, and she wondered if Sam was still there after all. She paused and tilted her head to see if she could hear what they were saying. If they were still fighting, she was going to go right back upstairs until they were done.

But it didn't take long to realize that it wasn't Sam she was talking to. And since there was only one voice, it had to be by phone, but by then she'd heard more than enough to catch her attention.

"I told you not to worry about it. It won't be much longer. The kid is desperate to have her mommy back and as soon as I get rid of the boyfriend, she'll do whatever I say. She only wants the ranch because she doesn't know anything else. When we get out of here, she'll change her mind and we'll figure out a way around the damn will."

Vicky sounded so cold and mocking. It was like being stabbed with an icicle and Charlie restrained the urge to storm downstairs and tell her off. She wanted to hear more first. Every word was confirming exactly what her father's letter had told her.

There was silence for a minute and then the sound of a dramatic sigh. "I haven't gotten much out of her yet, but I'll send you half. Try paying the bills with it instead of blowing it on junk. I'm not made of money and it's going to take time to get Charlie to turn over some of that inheritance to me. I'm working on it but if I go too fast even she'd get suspicious."

Charlie covered her mouth with both hands to block the angry words that wanted to pour out. She wasn't even crying, not this time. She'd used up all her tears on the letter. Now there was only a cold pit of anger coiling up tight in her stomach, ready to snap.

"It will be easier with her stupid hick boyfriend out of the picture. He's already run off. It's only a matter of time before he up and quits. I can't even imagine what she sees in him. Ugh."

And that was enough of that. If she heard one more vile word about Sam, she'd explode. She quietly backed up the stairs and then started down again with loud stomping footsteps to alert Vicky she was coming.

By the time she got to the bottom her mother was off the phone and looking in her direction with one of her perfectly (fake) smiles. "Hi baby, sorry about the fight. I just couldn't handle seeing him bossing you around. It really worries me that you let him control you like that. I mean—"

"It's okay, mom. I know. I should probably go talk to him though ... where did he go?" It took a major effort to keep her voice calm and she wasn't sure she quite managed it.

"I—well, I'm sorry honey. He said some nasty things about being sick of us, and then next thing I knew he was driving off like a maniac. I'm not entirely sure he's planning to come back." She reached out a hand and settled it gentle on Charlie's arm. "Maybe it's time to just let him go?"

Charlie didn't need to hide her upset. Vicky had given her the perfect reason to let her emotions show. "He—he left?"

"Oh, honey ... men are just—you really can't trust them to

stick around through the hard parts. But you have me now." She pulled Charlie into her arms, hugged her, and patted her back gently.

A few hours ago, it would have soothed her, but now Charlie felt nothing. She was distant from the manipulations. She could see Vicky choosing exactly what expression to wear. It was so obvious now that she wondered how she'd ever been fooled. She supposed it was because she'd wanted to be.

She gently untangled herself from Vicky's arms and stepped back. "Hey Mom? Can I ask you a question?"

"Of course you can, Charlie. That's what mothers are for. I'm still getting used to it but I—"

Charlie cut her off. "Why did you act like you didn't know Jimmy was dead when you showed up?"

"What?" Her head titled to the side with a complete look of confusion. "Because I didn't know. How could I have?"

"Wasn't the lawyer able to get ahold of you? Even so, I mean, you must have guessed when the money stopped coming, right?"

"Money? What? Charlie, I don't understand where all this is coming from." Vicky's dark eyes predictably filled with tears.

"The money dad was paying you to stay away for my whole life. The money you happily took to support your life-style when you gave up seeing me forever. If the lawyer couldn't find you then I guess you must have realized when the money dried up, huh?"

Her mother's expression crumbled, and she seemed to age ten years in front of her. For once there was no delicate dabbing at her eyes. The tears ran freely cutting streaks through the make-up. But it was still an act.

She must have known that it was over, but she made an effort to deny it even so. "You can't possibly believe I would

—Charlie, I love you. I always loved—it was your *father* who wanted me out of your life. I had no choice but to agree to his terms!" The words managed to sound both hurt and outraged at the same time.

Charlie wanted to laugh but it hurt too much. "Yeah. Well, I'm going to make you a new deal. We're not going to negotiate. I'll give you my terms, take it or leave it."

"Charlie, please. You don't understand what it was like. I hated it here. The animals, the dirt, none of it was what I thought it would be. I knew you'd be okay here. You always loved Jimmy more anyway." Vicky's expression was full of pleading for Charlie's understanding.

Maybe some of it was real, or maybe she was just sad she'd messed up her payday. Well, if that was the case she didn't need to worry. Charlie wasn't going to throw her out with nothing. Vicky was still her mother. She held up a hand to cut her off and the older woman went silent.

"I'm going to go and find Sam, and I want you gone by the time I get back. Leave your contact and bank info on the table. I'll go through my finances and set up a monthly stipend for you. I don't know what dad was paying you—" She paused and looked at Vicky expectantly.

Her mother looked down and named a number that seemed huge to Charlie, who had never felt wealthy, but if Jimmy had been able to afford it then she assumed she could probably carry it too. "I'll discuss it with my lawyer and see what I can do."

Vicky looked up and Charlie thought maybe, maybe she was finally seeing the woman's true emotions. There was sorrow there, but gratitude too, and a little resentment. "You're just like your father." The words were without heat, resigned.

"Yes, I am. I guess that's what happens when you grow up

without a mother around. I'll do my best to make sure you're okay, but I've got some rules."

The older woman laughed; it was a brittle sound. "Of course you do. I suppose you want me to go away and never come back."

"Not exactly." Charlie shook her head. She'd thought about it, but that wasn't what she really wanted. "I want you to go away and not come back until I *invite* you. I need time to cool down and think about everything that happened. But then ... I want—I'd like a chance to get to know you without the masks and hidden motivations, but there are going to be boundaries this time."

Charlie wasn't sure what Sam would think about that, but one thing hadn't changed. She did still want a relationship with her mother. It couldn't have all been fake. They'd spent too much time together for her to think Vicky had been in-character every moment.

She was judging the hell out of the woman right now, but nothing was ever as simple as it seemed. And her dad's letter, while warning her, had still shown an unexpected amount of fairness when he'd talked about Vicky. If he could be fair ... then so could she.

Vicky seemed shocked. "You really want that?"

Charlie took a deep breath, held it, and then let it out slowly with a nod. "I do. Vicky, I missed having you in my life growing up. I don't know if Dad was right or wrong in keeping you away. I know he thought it was for the best, and maybe it was, but I'm an adult now. We might never be super close, but I want to at least try to be friendly."

Her mother seemed so fragile in that moment. Her eyes were wide and glossy with tears. Make-up smeared a clown mask across her face, but there was a vulnerability in her expression. Hope.

Charlie might have been imagining it or seeing what she

wanted to see, but it didn't matter. She wasn't going to be fooled again and next time Vicky came back it would be on new terms. She felt confident that if they couldn't be friends, at least she could have the closure she needed to finally get past all her childhood issues.

"I'll see about setting up the money, and once I've had some time to think I'll be in contact with you." She hesitated and then leaned in and laid a gentle kiss on her mother's cheek. "Bye mom."

She didn't look back as she left. Vicky was her past, but Sam was her future and she needed to go make things right with him before it was too late.

CHAPTER 12

He hadn't planned on getting in a huge fight with her mother. He'd gone there with the sole intention of taking his girl home, even if he had to sling her over his shoulder and carry her there himself.

She wanted some space, so he'd given her three days. That was more than reasonable, but the whole point of her moving in had been to prove she was ready to commit. To be fair neither of them had expected to be tested like this, but he was her Dom. She couldn't just take off without talking to him.

The worst part was how obvious it was that she wanted to come home. He could see it in the way she leaned into him and looked off towards the ranch with a sad expression, but she wouldn't give in. He probably could have talked her into it if her mother hadn't come storming out.

He'd given up any pretense of liking Vicky. She was hurting Charlie. She was manipulative as hell, and whatever her plans where they were *not* in his girl's best interests. He'd still done his best to be polite to her for Charlie's sake, until she started insulting him and then it had escalated quickly.

The fight took up his entire focus, so he didn't actually notice Charlie staying out of it. He saw her as she ducked inside the house and let her go. It was probably better for her not to be in the middle of the mess, and he felt bad that he'd let Vicky goad him into losing his temper.

It couldn't be easy for her to watch her partner and mother fighting. But once she was gone, he stopped holding back and let Vicky have it with both barrels. "I don't know what you think you're doing here *Ms. Townsend*, but it's going to stop. I love Charlie too much to let you continue to take advantage of her."

"That's my daughter you're talking about, and she's too good for you. I can't believe she fell for a scruffy ranch hand, but believe me, once she sees what else is out there, she'll drop you in a hot second."

"Charlie and I grew up together. We've been friends since we were kids and nothing you can do is going to tear us apart," he retorted. His hands twitched and he balled them into fists. "If you really think Charlie wants some fancy boy with an office job and suit than you don't know her at all. She loves the ranch. She loves this life, and you might have her fooled right now, but she's going to see through you eventually."

She sniffed and tossed her hair back. "She doesn't know any better, not yet. But we've been talking about traveling. I'm going to show her there's more out there and when she sees it, she won't want to be held down here."

He couldn't help laughing. "Charlie knows plenty about what's out there. She went to college across the country, and then grad school. She's been on trips all over the country. She even went to Europe one summer. I don't know why you seem to think she's some naïve kid who's never been off the spread, but you're dead wrong. She's been out there, she saw it, and she still wanted this life."

Vicky looked taken aback, but then she shook it off. "College is different. It's not the real world."

Vicky didn't seem to know her daughter any better than Charlie knew her mother. It seemed like they each had an image of the other that just didn't match up to the reality. It would be funny if it wasn't going to end up hurting his girl.

"If you say so, but the fact is I know your daughter better than you do. She's happy here, or at least she was before you came. If you really care about her, you'll stop whatever you're doing and let her have the life she wants." He put every bit of cold Dom voice into the words. Not that he thought it would help, but he wanted her to know he was serious.

"Who are you to tell me how to treat my own daughter?" Vicky's voice was reaching screeching levels and it made his head hurt like nails on a blackboard. "You have no right! How dare you!"

He had a feeling Charlie wouldn't be happy if he pointed out that he was her Dom and responsible for her, though he was tempted. "I'm her partner and her friend, and I love her. That gives me the right."

She glared, practically shaking with anger. "You're just a field hand. You're not good enough for her and I'll make sure she sees that."

"Okay, you do that, lady. But in the meantime, I'd appreciate it if you kept your nose out of the ranch. If I hear you've been calling around and asking if anyone wants to buy it, you and I are gonna have some words you won't like. Legal ones." It was partly a bluff. He didn't really have any proof and wasn't entirely sure what she'd done was against the law anyway.

The furniture sale had definitely been sketchy, but Charlie had already forgiven that, and he had no legal authority over the house, only the ranch. But he wanted to see how she reacted to him throwing it out there like he knew for sure it was her.

He wasn't disappointed. The shocked, pinched look on her face said it all. She stammered out denials, but they didn't sound authentic. He just cocked a half smile, one eyebrow up like he was amused that she was even trying.

It seemed to set her off and soon there wasn't even a hint of composure. He had to admit he'd done it on purpose just to see what she'd do when she lost control. He was hoping she'd slip up and admit to her real intentions.

Instead, she started throwing out insults that lacked any subtlety at all, and eventually he snapped back. He should have put a stop to it then and left, but maybe it was time for it to all come to a head. Still, the slap took him by surprise and for a second they both stared at each other.

He might have deserved it. He'd been so angry he wasn't even sure what he'd said, but it had probably been mean. Next thing he knew Vicky's hand lashed out and slapped him hard. His head rocked back, and his own hand had come up instantly in response.

It hovered there for a second and then he let it drop. "Keep your hands to yourself. Next time you hit me I'll return the favor," he said coldly. He'd never hit a woman in anger. Never hit one outside of the consensual kind of slapping that had a very different tone to it, but he was sorely tempted at the moment.

He turned on his heel and stalked away before he gave in to that temptation, calling over his shoulder, "Tell Charlie I'm going to get a hotel room for the night, so I can calm down."

Maybe she'd give her daughter the message, or maybe she wouldn't. He didn't trust her so when he swung by the cabin to grab some things, he left a quick note on the table. That way if Charlie came looking, she wouldn't worry. Then he tossed a duffle bag in the front seat of his truck and took off.

There weren't a lot of choices for accommodations in town. If he felt like making a drive, there was a fancy one near the freeway offramp that picked up all the tourist trade. But it was the seedy local motel down the road that he headed for. People joked that it was always easy to get a room there because most people only used it for an hour or two.

It wasn't terrible though. The units were worn but clean, and stocked with the usual amenities. The widow who ran it added homey little touches that you didn't normally find in a cheap motel. When he checked in, he left the office with an ancient plastic keychain holding a metal key, and a plate full of fresh homemade chocolate chip cookies. The cookies were definitely worth the price of letting her talk his ear off for a full fifteen minutes.

He'd already eaten two by the time he moved his truck down to the unit on the end. "Lucky number thirteen... that's not ominous or anything," he muttered as he tried to balance the duffle and the plate so he could unlock the door.

He dropped his bag on the bed and sighed. He'd hoped to be home right now with Charlie in his arms, not looking at peeling wallpaper that had to be at least fifty years old. But a little space between him and Vicky wasn't a terrible thing. He still couldn't believe she'd slapped him.

The whole situation made him tired. His head was pounding from a tension headache and he was tempted to flop on the bed and go to sleep. Instead, he stripped and headed for the shower. The steam would help, and he planned to use up every drop of hot water.

But like most of his plans, things fell apart. Fifteen minutes in, with the bathroom shrouded in billowing clouds of steam, there was a knock on the door to his room. He assumed it was a mistake and ignored it, but it came again, longer and louder. At that point he started wondering if it was an angry husband who had the wrong room. If so, it would probably be better to ignore it.

But then he thought about Charlie. Her mother might have told her after all, or she might have seen the note saying he was getting a room for the night and it wasn't like there were many choices. He shut off the water and yelled, "One second!" through the open doorway.

He grabbed a towel with a fraying hem from a stack on the sink and wrapped it around his waist as he left the bathroom. The idea of answering the door for an angry lover, dressed in nothing but a towel, wasn't that appealing but by then the knocking was almost nonstop. He was beginning to worry that any neighbors hoping for a romantic nooner were going to be seriously pissed by the noise. "I'm coming, damn it!"

He actually paused to laugh as he thought about how many times the walls had probably heard *that* particular phrase—though with an entirely different context. Might even have heard it from him or Charlie. Back in the day they'd had occasion to slip away and grab a room together. Even though he'd had his own place on the ranch it hadn't always been easy getting the privacy with her dad around.

He was still amused when he yanked open the door so suddenly that Charlie stumbled forward, hand still raised to bang again. He caught and steadied her. "Charlie, damn girl, you—"

"Sam, just listen, okay? Please, I know you're really pissed, and I don't blame you," she said. The words blurted as if she was trying to get them in fast.

"I'm not p—"

"Please, just give me a chance to talk, okay?" Her dark eyes, just like her mother's down to the shape and color, filled with tears.

Despite the physical similarities he was struck for a

moment by how different they looked. Where Vicky's were cold and seemed to be shaded with secrets and machinations, Charlie's were warm and showed every emotion.

"Okay, you've got the floor." He stepped back to let her into the room so he could close the door. He doubted the reputation of the Hideaway could get any worse, but half-naked men standing in doorways probably wasn't going to help much.

He took a seat on the end of the bed and watched as she began to pace back and forth. The pure nervous energy she was exuding had his skin stippling with goosebumps. After several minutes of silence, he cleared his throat to get her attention. "Are you going to talk or just wear a hole in the carpet?"

She stopped short. "Sorry. I just ... I was afraid you wouldn't even give me a chance to talk, and then I wanted to make sure I said everything right." She took a deep breath, visibly pulling herself together.

"I guess ... I need to start with apologizing. I'm so sorry. You were right. You were right about everything and I should have listened. I wanted—I wanted so much for her to be the way I'd dreamed her all my life that I didn't want to hear what you were saying." She looked down, hands clasped together, fingers twisting, as if the energy simply had to find a new outlet.

"Charlie, I get—"

"Please!" Her head snapped up, cutting him off and he sighed and waved for her to go on. "You're my Daddy and I should have listened to you. By not taking what you said into account I disrespected that relationship, as well as the romantic one. And then I moved out. That was the worst thing. I should never—I promised I was done with running, but then I ran." Her voice shook. Tears started to track down her cheeks.

It was taking everything he had not to interrupt her and pull her into his arms. His hands knotted in the towel and there was a small tearing sound as the worn old thing ripped from the tension.

"I just thought that if I stayed up at the house with her, she'd settle down, and you two wouldn't fight. It was only going to be a couple of weeks, but I should have at least talked to you first. And I deserve any punishment you want to give me, but please, please don't leave me Sam. Please come home."

Towards the end the words burst from her like a plea and he realized that she thought he had left for good. Not for a night away from the ranch to cool down, but permanently. Although his first instinct was to drag her into his lap and reassure her that he'd always planned to come back, he didn't.

There were a few things he wanted to know first. "You said I was right. That must mean you figured something out about Vicky. Want to tell me about it?"

"Oh—fuck. Right. You need to read this." She fumbled in her pocket and pulled out a folded, worn-looking envelope and handed it to him.

Both eyebrows went up as he reached for it. "Is this the letter from Jimmy?"

She nodded.

He unfolded it carefully and smoothed it out in his lap. "You sure you want me to read this?"

"Yes. I wish—oh, why didn't I read it after the funeral? It would have saved so much trouble. Damn it." She pounded her thigh with a closed fist, hard enough that it had to hurt.

He frowned. "Knock that off, before you bruise yourself." It was difficult not to add "If anyone is going to bruise your thighs it will be me," but he was trying to play it cool until everything was sorted. "And have a seat. I can't read this if you're bouncing all over the place."

She perched on the edge of the bed next to him, and watched as he pulled the letter out of the envelope and began to read. By the time he was done, he was wishing he'd insisted she read the letter earlier too—or at least suggested it strongly. He understood the many reasons why she'd put it off but if they'd known about Vicky from the start things would have gone very differently when she showed up.

"Well. What are you going to do about her now?" he asked, one eyebrow going up in question. It was still going to have to be her choice unless she asked him to make it for her. He was sticking to that.

"It's done. I told her to pack and go before I left to come find you." She said it simply, without looking up at him. Her eyes were fixed on her hands as they rested in her lap.

He kept his voice neutral. "You sure it was a good idea to leave her there? I mean I wouldn't trust her not to clear the house of any valuables on her way out."

"Well..." There she was gnawing at her lip again. It would be a bloody mess before she was done. She was worried about telling him something and he wanted to know what it was.

"Charlie?"

"She won't do anything else because if she does, she won't get the money I promised her." She snuck a nervous look in his direction and then flinched away when she found him watching her.

He was confused, stunned really, but he wanted to understand. "After you found all this out, why would you give her anything?" He tried to be gentle with the question, but he wasn't sure if he was successful.

"It's just ... she's not all bad. There were a lot of things that I think were real. I do think she loves me. Even Dad thought so." She waved her hand at the letter.

"Yes, but he also made it clear he didn't think you were ever the top of her list."

"I don't need to be, especially not now after all these years. It was nice having a mom, getting to live out all those fantasies I had as a kid, but I don't really need to be the focus of anyone's world, except yours."

He so badly wanted to wrap an arm around her when she said that. As if she could ever not be the most important thing in his life. Even before he'd become her Daddy, she'd meant everything to him. He really didn't see that changing any time soon.

"Maybe you better tell me what you promised her, Charlie. All of it." He used a little of his Dom voice there to help her push past the nerves. He wanted to wrap this up, so he could hold her and a lot of stammering and pussy footing around the truth wasn't conducive to that.

"Well, I—" She took one look at the hard expression on his face and spit it all out. "I told her to leave her contact and bank info. I'd look into my finances and see if I could afford to send her about what dad was. I mean that seemed fair. He's been paying her all this time, and it couldn't just be because of me. I was gone at school for years. He could have stopped then and she wouldn't have been able to find me."

She sounded hesitant, that note of waiting for his approval hung on every word, but he let it dangle. "In exchange for her staying away?"

"No. No, not exactly..." She trailed off. Her nerves were ramping up he could see it.

He made his voice harder, "Charlie. All of it."

"She's not allowed to come back until she's invited, but I did tell her that at some point ... when I—we were ready, we'd invite her back." She hastened to add, "But I told her there were going to be boundaries and limits next time she came and none of this sneaky stuff."

Oh, hell no.

He sighed and bit back the urge to say it out loud. That was not what he'd wanted to hear at all. Not after the woman had caused so much trouble, but he could kind of see Charlie's side. She was trying to keep the lines open. He couldn't blame her for that.

Well, he could ... but it wouldn't do any good. Feelings were ridiculously illogical and when it came to parents, he supposed a blind spot was normal.

But when it actually came around to inviting her, he was going to enforce those boundaries hard. He wasn't going through this again. He wasn't about to let Charlie put up with being pulled back and forth between the two of them. Once was enough.

"You really think she'll behave herself next time?"

Charlie shrugged. "I think she better if she wants to keep getting her monthly check. If Jimmy was right and she puts herself first, then I guess she'll toe the line to keep the money flowing. If she does anything like this again my interest in keeping the relationship open is going to die." Her voice made an attempt at being cold.

It didn't quite make it, but he gave her points for trying. "As long as you stick with that, I guess things will be okay then. No timeline on when you'd be inviting her back? Just sometime in the future?"

She nodded. "It's going to take me a while to get over this. See, after I read the letter, I went down to confront her, and accidentally overheard her on the phone." She closed her eyes and shook her head. "I heard enough. Enough to know you were right the whole time and I was an idiot for not listening to you."

"And now that you heard the truth from her own mouth,

and from your father—now you actually believe me? That's reassuring, so next time I won't have to track down a notary to get a sworn statement I just have to force the truth out of people, and then you'll listen?" The words tinged on sarcastic, but he didn't allow any emotion to show on his face as he watched her.

Her bottom lip trembled. "I shouldn't have needed that. She was a stranger and I let myself be swayed by a blood relationship. You're the one I know and trust. If you forgive me and come back, I promise—" The tears were starting to run faster, pouring down her cheeks.

"Did she at least give you the message that I went to the hotel?"

Charlie shook her head and frowned. "No—I just figured where else would you go? If you weren't here, I was going to try the big hotel, but this one was closer." Suddenly her eyes were on his and she was grabbing at his hand and holding it. "I know I don't deserve it Sam, but I need you to come home. Please? I promise I'll be better."

Maybe he was an asshole for not comforting her right there, and explaining the whole situation, but for his own peace of mind there was one last thing he needed to know. Charlie wasn't the only one who had doubts sometimes. Not about her, not about them, but sometimes he did worry in the back of his head that her need for him to stay with the ranch overrode her actual need for him as her lover and Daddy.

He'd never tried to play it against her. He'd always wanted her to believe that he would do his best to make sure she kept the spread no matter how their relationship stood. But back in those turbulent days right after the will had been read, he'd almost walked out and when she begged him to stay it had been to save the ranch. Sometimes the memory of that messed with his head.

"Well, I wouldn't want you to lose the ranch just because I left."

She stared at him wide-eyed. "Fuck the ranch, Sam. *You're* what I need!"

He snorted. That was maybe a little too dramatic to be real. "Fuck the ranch? *Really*? You'd be fine with losing it?"

She took a gulping breath and blew it out with a laugh. "Of course not. I'm crazy in love with you, but I'm not stupid. I've got enough money in investments to buy it back if the lawyer sold it because you left. I'd hire someone to buy it by proxy if necessary, and half the money would come back to me after the sale anyway. I figured out months ago that I could get around that clause in the will pretty easily. I'm sure Jimmy knew I would too. He just wanted me to have time to settle down and accept the situation before I got to the solution."

That meant something. He'd probably have to unpack it all later when things settled, but it did put to rest the one real concern he'd had over their relationship. He wanted Charlie, but not if she felt like she was held hostage by him. Knowing that she'd already worked that part out and was really truly with him out of love meant a lot.

"Then you came after me because..."

"Because I love you, and I want to spend the rest of my life with you. And Vicky said— Vicky said you probably weren't coming back. When she said that I felt like all the air had been sucked out of the room. I can't live without you Sam. So, I don't care about the punishment, I just need you to come back with me."

He looked at her thoughtfully and she stared back with hope and fear all over her face. "You make a compelling case, Charlie. But the thing is ... I was never planning on leaving for good. I just needed to get as far from your mother as possible before I lost my temper. And to be honest I didn't want to spend another night in our bed without you. I was coming back in the morning."

Her eyes went wide and round. "Really?"

"Really. I tried to tell you I wasn't mad when you got here, but you insisted I wait until you had your say first." The words were gentle, and he pulled her into his lap as he said them.

She wrapped her arms around him and clung to his bare skin. "I just thought ... I wouldn't have blamed you if ..."

"I left a note on the table at home explaining, but I guess you never got that far." She shook her head without looking up. "Vicky was supposed to tell you I was leaving for the night, but I guess she twisted it for her own agenda."

"I messed everything up, Daddy. I can't believe I fell for all of her games." She sounded so miserable. She sniffled and then snuck a quick glance up at his face. "Are you sure you're not mad at me?"

That lost little girl tone was heavy in her voice and all he wanted to do was hold her and never let her go. Of course, there was still the matter of the punishment to deal with. There was so much guilt there that he could hear it weighing her down and she wouldn't feel better until it was addressed.

He couldn't blame her for wanting a relationship with her mother, or for putting her trust in the woman who *should* have wanted to love and protect Charlie above everyone else. Those were natural things, and he had no idea how he would have reacted in her position.

There was some annoyance that she hadn't listened to him. She'd been too close to the problem and couldn't see clearly, but that was supposed to be his job—to help her when she couldn't find the right path on her own. But no, he wasn't mad at her for it.

Moving out of their house with just a note on the table though ... that was still chafing and definitely called for punishment. As for the rest, he didn't think punishment was justified, but it didn't really matter what he thought. She felt guilty; she regretted her choices, and she was miserable over them.

As her Daddy it was his job to clear that up for her. She needed the punishment to wipe the slate clean so she could move forward, so *they* could move forward without baggage.

"I'm sure I'm not mad... but I'm also sure my little girl needs to be punished. The only thing you did that actually disappointed me was creeping out of our home without a word. It hurt, coming home to find that letter. You have no idea how close I was to storming over there and tossing you over my shoulder to carry you home."

"Probably would have been better if you had."

"Naw, I doubt that. There are always going to be some decisions I can't make for you, darlin'. Dom, Daddy, or partner, there are going to be some choices that only you can decide. I don't always like it, and I'm betting you don't either, but that's the way it is."

She buried her face against his neck and sighed. "I guess."

He chuckled. "Charlie, I know you. You wouldn't be happy if I took complete control of you. You need taming, but you're always going to be a wild spirit. It's one of the things I love about you. It's not my job to take away your right to choose. All I can do is guide you."

"I love it when you take total control in the bedroom, but you're right, I'd go crazy if you did it all the time. It's just hard sometimes to balance everything. I want to submit to you, but I also want to be strong and independent."

"It will get easier, I think. Eventually we'll be in a place where you can make peace with both sides of you. They aren't incompatible, you know." He rubbed her back gently, inhaled the sweet scent of her shampoo and sighed. "I missed you, baby."

"I missed you too. It didn't feel like three days. It felt like weeks. It was dumb moving over to the big house like that and I knew it as soon as I got there. I guess it was partly pride that made me stay. After leaving that dramatic letter I couldn't just turn around and come back."

"Pride can make things harder all around. I understood why you wanted so badly to believe in your mother, but my ego was stung that you didn't listen to me. I knew, logically, that you weren't really choosing between us, but emotions are trickier, and it still hurt."

"I promise I wasn't choosing her over you. I swear, Daddy. I was just mixed up. Scared she'd leave and I'd lose the only chance to know her." Her voice broke halfway through. She started to sob and once that happened it seemed like the tears would never stop. It wasn't a quiet cry, and it was hard to listen to the raw wrenching pain in them, and there wasn't much he could do about it but hold her.

It seemed to go on forever until finally she began to hiccup. The tears slowed as she tried to get the hiccups under control. The act of holding her breath seemed to help with both. She calmed slowly and finally could talk again. "I j-just wanted it to be real, Daddy. I wanted it so bad. I never meant t-t-to h-hurt you."

The idea that he'd been hurt seemed to make her shrink in his arms. He felt hot tears rolling down his bare back as he held her. He rocked her slowly. "I know, baby, but being the Dom doesn't give me perfect confidence. It poked at my doubts, and I started wondering if you were only with me because of the ranch. So, when you showed up … I guess I needed to know."

She was silent for a second. "We—we should get married." She blurted the words, quick like she might change her mind.

Sam froze, eyes widening and his arms around her stiffened. It was the last thing he'd ever expected her to say. He cleared his throat. "That some kind of proposal?"

She pushed back, sitting up straight to look at him. "Yes, why not. Will you marry me Daddy?" Her eyes were red and swollen but she seemed sincere.

He didn't know what to say. Of course he wanted to marry her. He'd wanted to marry her since they were teenagers, but this wasn't what he'd expected when he'd pictured the proposal happening. He discarded his first reaction to say yes, and then his second, which was to treat it like a joke.

This needed a serious reply because while it showed amazing growth on working through her commitment issues, it was definitely not the time. "Charlie, nothing would make me happier than for us to get married," he said carefully.

He took a deep breath and shook his head feeling a strong sense of regret. "But I don't think now is the best time to make this commitment. You, darlin', are struggling with a lot of wild emotions and trying to deal with some trauma. I think—I think this is more about you really wanting to reassure me that you love me, am I right?"

She nodded slowly. There was no sign of panic from the discussion of marriage and no obvious emotions to let him know how she was handling the gentle rejection. He hoped he wasn't making things worse.

"Alright, so how about this. We're going to table this for today. I want you to take some time to think about this. Then, in a couple months or so if you still want to get married, you can propose again. Or if you decide you want to do things the traditional way you just let me know and I'll get down on one knee for you. Is that fair?"

Tension drained from her body, showing she hadn't been quite as calm about the discussion as she'd looked, but a slight smile curved her lips at one corner. "That's fair and... it might be nice having *you* on your knees, for a change." The smile turned into a smirk.

He snorted. "One knee. You get *one* knee and if you smirk when I'm down there I'll put you across it—right after I ask the question."

She couldn't hold back the laughter at that point. Shaking her head as she rolled her eyes. "Fine, it was just a thought."

"Uh huh. Keep those thoughts in check, little girl. They'll get you in trouble. Speaking of trouble ... we've got the other issue to deal with. Part of moving forward is clearing the slate. You know what that means?" He let his voice grow harder towards the end, hinting.

She frowned and nodded. "You're going to spank me?" There was hesitation, as if hoping she was wrong.

"Yep."

She looked around nervously. "Here?"

"Why not? It wouldn't be the weirdest thing to happen in this room I'm sure. Wouldn't you like to get it over with?"

"I'd rather the whole motel didn't hear me getting spanked through these thin walls." There was just a little bit of sass to the words.

She did have a point. The walls were pretty thin, and he wasn't too interested in getting a domestic disturbance call put in on them. Nothing ruined a good day like the police showing up to make sure the whuppin' was consensual.

"Hmm, suppose we can put it off until we get home. Might be for the best since I don't have anything but my hand to use here, and I'm thinking this discussion might call for some extra oomph. Maybe that new mean toy I just got in the mail."

Charlie's expression shifted as she realized she'd just made things harder for herself, but before she could change her mind, he threw a distraction her way.

"Of course, I do have this room paid for the night and it would be a shame to waste it. If I'm not going to paddle your butt, I guess we'll have to think of something else to do."

She perked up immediately. "I have an idea about that!"

He laughed. "I bet you do." He pulled her closer. His mouth came down hard on hers and as the kiss extended, he collapsed backwards on the bed and pulled her with him. His hand slid up her leg, pushing the skirt up as it moved underneath to find her panties.

She hadn't dressed for seduction and the plain white cotton looked innocent against her tan skin. It invited a slap, and he brought his palm down hard across the rounded hill of her ass and then tightened his hand to grip the cheek possessively. He didn't need to say the word *mine*; they both knew what it meant.

He shoved her thighs apart with one leg and pressed his knee up against the crotch of her panties. He could feel the wetness of her interest already starting to soak through and he encouraged it by landing another spank.

She rocked forward with a low moan, grinding against his knee. Her mouth caught his, kissing him with a furious hunger that couldn't be ignored. Fingers twined in his hair, holding him until finally she broke away breathless.

He looked at her as his fingers slipped under the elastic of the panties and caressed the soft warm flesh where he'd just spanked. "No more running away." The words were harsh, not with anger but something more primal than that.

"No Daddy, no more running," she promised. Maybe it was true, maybe it wasn't, but in that moment, she meant it and the was good enough for him.

When he'd tipped them over, the towel had pulled loose and now his growing erection was nudging against her bare thigh. She reached down and wrapped her hand around his length, stroking and teasing, while his tongue played with hers. It was easy to let the world slip away. Her mouth, her hands, her body pressed against his became his focus.

He undressed her, fumbling and tugging in frustration as she laughed and tried to help. He growled and pushed her hands away. "I'll do it," he said, and then cursed when the skirt twisted around her waist and he couldn't get to the buttons to release it.

After a minute of aggressively muttering as he tried to untangle it, he finally gave up and gave it a sharp yank. With a ripping sound the waist tore loose.

"Hey!"

"Oh, hush. You don't need it anymore. Now that your mother's gone, you'll be back in jeans anyway." He wasn't dumb and knew very well why Charlie's style had suddenly changed to match Vicky's more ladylike ways.

It had been strange seeing her in skirts and dresses all the time. Not that they didn't have their uses. The easy access for starters. But it had been another of many changes he'd seen being forced on her.

"Yeah, but ... what am I going to wear home?" She tried to sound put out, but she was too excited to manage it and he saw right through the act.

"We'll worry about that later. Maybe we'll tuck you into one of my shirts. They're long enough on you." He gave the skirt another yank and then wrestled the shredded fabric off and tossed it aside.

The panties were going to be a different level of difficulty and he had to remove his knee from its warm nest between her thighs. But first he collected another kiss. His tongue invaded her mouth, exploring. Both hands squeezed and massaged her ass at the same time. When he got around to removing her underwear they were thoroughly soaked, and she was begging for more.

He wanted to sink into the sweet heat of her body right

then, but forced himself to wait, drawing it out for both of them. Besides, he wanted to see her completely naked first. The blouse was easy to deal with, it unbuttoned in the front. The bra was slightly more complicated, but he managed to get it unhooked.

She sprawled across the bed and looked at him with such love that it took his breath away. Often their sex was rough, hard and fast to match the passion coursing through them, but in that moment, he wanted to make love to her slowly. He wanted to watch her face as she came undone.

He sensed she felt the same. They needed this slow gentle touching now, the same way they'd needed the frenzied coupling on his office desk a few weeks before. Neither of them was in a hurry to push things to the conclusion because they were too wrapped up in the moment.

CHAPTER 13

There had been so many emotions rushing through her as she left the house and headed straight to her car. Fear topped the list. She'd made so many mistakes with Sam and after everything that had gone down, she worried she'd finally messed things up so bad he'd be out the door.

Under that was a feeling of being completely stupid. She'd been suspicious when Vicky first arrived but somewhere along the way she'd gagged those skeptical worries and buried them in the back of her mind. The fantasy was so enticing to the little girl who had always missed her mom.

Of course it was so clear and obvious now, but she'd let her emotions get the best of her. It wasn't a new fault. But ignoring the people she trusted, that had been the worst part of it, and she wasn't sure how Sam would be able to forgive her this time.

Finding him wouldn't be hard. It was a small town. There were only two places to stay and likely he'd go to the closest one so at least she knew where to go first. The joints of her fingers were white from how hard she gripped the steering wheel, and she paid minimal attention to driving, so she was probably lucky to make it there safely.

But the quiet backroads were good places to think and she spent the ten-minute drive focused entirely on what she was going to say to Sam when she got there. Apologies would come first, of course. And she might as well suggest punishment right off the bat, so he knew she was completely aware that this had been her screw-up.

It wasn't lost on her that if he did come back home with her, punishment would probably be a pretty high priority anyway and her butt tightened reflexively in the seat. She was really going to be in for it—but it didn't matter. She would take any punishment as long as he didn't give up on her.

Just the thought of that started her trembling and she had to pull over to get a grip on the overwhelming panic. Making it worse was this fear that every second's delay could somehow make it worse. She needed to see him immediately to fix it, but the pressure to hurry up and calm down had the opposite effect.

It took her a while to realize she was causing a spiral and start backing down. It ended with a spate of tears, but those at least she could cut off. She needed to cry, but not yet. Not until she found Sam and knew things would be okay. Then she could finally let herself break a little.

She pulled back onto the road and drove straight to the motel. She didn't need to check at the desk. His truck was there, parked at the end in front of the last unit. It took her a minute to gather her courage before she knocked on the door. When there was no answer she knocked again, harder.

The desperate need to see him, to talk to him, translated into a frenzied banging on the door. Even when he called out to say he was coming, she couldn't make her hand stop hammering. He opened the door so abruptly that she fell forward into his arms.

It felt so good to be there, even if it was only for a moment while he steadied her. As much as she wanted to cling to him and hold onto that feeling for a little longer, she felt like she needed to get all her apologies and explanations out quickly. She was afraid of what he had to say to her, so she cut him off, begging him to let her speak first.

He stepped back to let her enter the room and then waited for her to have her say. The carefully planned script vanished from her mind and she had a feeling she ended up babbling, but it didn't matter. It might have been disorganized but in the end, she got it all out.

It hadn't been so bad. He hadn't even been angry that she'd left the door cracked on her relationship with her mother. She'd really worried about that.

But hearing his response to all of it wasn't easy. Knowing that he'd been hurt, that he'd started to feel insecure because of the choices she made was painful. She understood it, but she'd gotten so used to thinking of him as the stable half of their partnership. She'd forgotten that things might not be easy for him either.

Even Daddies could have doubts, who knew? She felt horrible to have caused them. The suggestion that they get married seemed to come out of nowhere. Just weeks ago, the very word had set her on the edge of panicking, but somehow that had changed. Maybe she'd grown and getting some kind of resolution with her mother, even if it wasn't the kind she wanted, had helped her with those commitment issues.

It was more likely that the shock of thinking she might lose him had shaken her up enough to realize how much she needed forever with this man. If marriage wiped away the hurt she'd caused, then she'd willingly walk down the aisle. There was still a small sense of relief when he suggested they wait a few months. Maybe it would take a bit longer to completely get past her baggage.

The important thing was that they were going to move forward together, and she felt the last of the fear and tension going out of her. It left her shaky, weak, but relieved enough to tease him a little. And as embarrassing as it would have been to be spanked in a motel with paper thin walls, she would have accepted it as something she'd earned. Waiting until they got home was much better though, even if it did mean Sam had access to the meaner toys.

She was glad to put all thought of punishment off in favor of *other* activities. He began to kiss her as his hand explored her body. It was a gentle loving, full of soft touches and caresses.

She let go of everything just to concentrate on him and what he was doing to her. It was so nice to say goodbye to the stress and fears she'd been living with. Her conscious mind drifted in a pleasant haze as she relaxed entirely for the first time in ages. At least her mind did. Her body was far from limp and relaxed. It was hyper-attuned to everything that was happening.

The occasional spank just added to her enjoyment as it always did, but the ripping of her skirt did pull her briefly back to the present. She pretended to be upset but she wasn't really. Having the clothes ripped from her body was hot and although there was the worry of what she would wear home —that was future Charlie's problem, and she was happy to toss it away like he tossed the remains of her skirt.

He stripped her naked with a single-minded focus and then he began to kiss, lick, and bite his way around her body. It seemed like every inch of her skin felt the touch of his mouth in one way or another, and he wasn't half through before she was gasping and moaning. He had yet to reach between her thighs and she was already panting with need.

When he finally worked his way down between her legs, dropping light kisses on her inner thighs, she was nearly desperate. Her back arched up off the bed, lifting her sex in a silent plea for more. Fingers, mouth, or cock, she didn't care but she needed his attention focused *there*.

He spread her legs, gripping her upper thighs and chuckled as he leaned in to blow a soft breath across the damp curls. He deliberately held back what she needed just to tease her. He took his time, drawing things out until she was ready to scream. She could hear a soft whimpered pleading, and suddenly realized it was her.

"Please Daddy, please touch me. Please I need—I need you to touch me."

"I *am* touching you, darlin'. Can't you feel it?" He tightened his grip on both legs and nipped her inner thigh playfully.

She couldn't hold back the whine, or the exasperated, "Not there, Daddy!"

"No?" He leaned in and dragged his tongue across the soft flesh just below her belly button. "How about here?"

"Maybe a little further down," she said as she lifted her hips. Her attempt to guide him to the exact spot where she wanted his attention just seemed to amuse him.

"Maybe you better tell me *exactly* what you want. Otherwise, I might never get it right—and this will be a good chance for you to practice your communication skills."

It was a very light admonishment and when she looked down, she could see that he was mostly just teasing her. His eyes twinkled and she caught sight of a slight grin curving his mouth before his face vanished so he could go back to kissing and licking her skin everywhere but where she wanted him.

She knew he wanted her to spell it out in graphic terms. Sometimes when she was feeling bold, she had no problem with dirty talk. Other times, like today, there was something uniquely embarrassing about lewd talk. She squirmed in his grasp.

The vulnerability of their earlier conversation hadn't completely vanished yet. She could still feel it and that made it a struggle to use the words he wanted. "Please, Daddy, please. You know what I want." She reached down and tried to show him, stroking the place that badly needed his attention.

"Use your words, Baby. Tell me what you want." His tone was encouraging and for added incentive he pushed her legs open a little wider, and then freed his hands so he could part the plump lower lips. He spread them and leaned in close, so his warm breath tickled across the glistening folds.

She let out a long shuddering breath. "Oh god … I'm going to die if you keep teasing me."

He laughed. "How long I tease is up to you, baby. I'm ready when you are."

Her face flushed with embarrassment and she closed her eyes so that seeing him sprawled between her thighs grinning didn't add to it. Why was it so easy sometimes and then other times nearly impossible? But she had no doubt that he meant what he said, and he'd continue to drive her crazy until she gave in.

Fuck it. She couldn't hold out anymore. "Lick me. Lick my pussy and finger me until I come." She lifted her hips as she said it, almost demanding he comply, but then added, "Please!" as an afterthought. She could feel an embarrassed heat rising up her neck as she said the words.

Maybe it was the demanding tone that made him push it just a little further. He drew his tongue up through the soaked folds and stopped just at her clit. She ground up against his mouth and got a little bit of the friction she badly needed but only for a second before he pulled back.

"Say 'Please, Daddy.' And tell me what a good girl you're going to be if I give you what you want." It wasn't a suggestion. The excitement was clear in his voice but under that was iron.

Her hands fisted in the comforter beneath her. A wet patch was forming underneath as her pussy spasmed with desire. "Please Daddy. I'll be soooo good. I'm going to be such a good girl. Your good girl. Yours. Please, please make me come."

He didn't take the time to praise her for obeying, or tease her any further, but he continued to keep it slow at first. Face buried in her slick heat, he lapped at her. She couldn't think of anything but his tongue and how good it felt. Her fingers threaded through his hair and she grabbed a handful and held on as her need coiled up tight inside of her.

He had to know she was on the edge of breaking because finally he changed it up. Slow and easy turned into licking, stroking, and sucking like he was ravenous, and she was a buffet only for him. Her body was so primed and ready that she came in under a minute, but he didn't stop. He didn't even slow down.

Everything went over-sensitive and she whimpered as she tried to push him away. But he pinned her in place, batted her hands out of the way and continued until she was writhing on his tongue and crying out with no concern for the neighbors. When she came a second time, he slid two fingers into her and hooked them as he began to finger her.

No, she'd been wrong earlier. He was going to kill her,

but it wouldn't be from the waiting; it would be from this. This intense, over-the-top pleasure that was rolling through her body until every muscle was tight and shaky. One cry after another filled the room. She begged and pleaded without knowing what she was asking for.

For him to stop? For him to continue? She couldn't separate them in her head. All she knew was she was coasting along on an endless wave of pleasure and when he finally covered her body and worked his shaft into her, she lost track of everything. Like a wild thing she wrapped her legs around his waist and rocked up to meet his thrusts.

Her nails clawed at his back. Their mouths met brutally, and her crushed lips stung. But the small pain was brief and washed away as she climaxed again. Spots swam in front of her eyes as her entire body arched into a bow. Her pussy clenched around his shaft milking him greedily until he stiffened and groaned.

She could feel him trying to hold out, trying to continue but his body overruled him. She watched his face as he managed one last shaking thrust and then shattered. Normally her eyes were closed by the time they reached this part. She found it easier to lose herself in the sensations without the distraction of watching their bodies move.

But now she opened her eyes just in time to see the intense concentration break apart into a look of pure wonder, and satisfaction filled his face. His head dropped, and their eyes met. They didn't need any words. The love that was reflected in each other's eyes said it all and it left no room for doubts.

Everything was going to be okay. She was his. He was hers. Together they would work through all the problems and their relationship would be stronger for it.

The End

(Don't forget to look for the next book in the series later this
year.)

ABOUT THE AUTHOR

Kessily Lewel, and her darker side Sadie Marks, are two halves of the same author. Between those pen names, she has a total of eleven published books and has participated in several anthologies. All of her work falls under the category of power-exchange romance. Kessily's books tend more towards sexy romance with a side of domestic discipline, while Sadie has been sticking to sci-fi, with her race of Dominant aliens who are looking for a few good humans to call their own.

She has been in love with fantasy, sci-fi and horror since she was a child. She grew up reading Stephen King, Asimov, Robert Heinlein, and others, so it was only natural that one day she'd write her own worlds—though hers *do* seem to have a lot more sex and BDSM in them.

The easiest way to find Kessily Lewel and Sadie Marks is through their blog and website: Kessilylewel.com

There you will find links to all their books and social media accounts.

Newsletter

Have you signed up for my newsletter yet?

If you enjoy a little (or a lot of) kink with your romance, then you should definitely subscribe to my newsletter. It's a nice compact way to find out what I'm up to under both pen names. Believe me, I've got a lot going on right now that you'll find interesting!

Plus, rotating free stuff to make it even more fun. Right now, you'll get a free copy of my last release, *Architect of His Desire* just for signing up. So, grab it now before you miss your chance.

Each month it will hit your in-box with:

Monthly news
Teasers
Upcoming events
New releases
Free stuff
And offerings from other hot authors

Chaotic Musings Newsletter Sign-up
https://kessilylewel.com/newsletter/

Did you miss the first in the Daddy Takes the Reins series?

A rekindled romance. A second chance at love. The Daddy she needs.

Claiming His Brat
Daddy Takes the Reins Book One

A loud knock at the door pulled him out of his thoughts. Before he could reply it opened, and the grizzled head of his second in command poked around the edge looking nervous. "Hey, uh, Sam? We might have a problem out here."

He sighed. "What is it now, Ben? If it's Jeff, you can tell him to hit the road—"

Ben shook his head rapidly, and the door inched open a little further. "No. It's Charlie. She's decided to spend some time with one of the horses."

Sam cocked his head, eyes narrowing. "And why is that a problem?" It didn't take long for the other shoe to drop; he knew Ben wouldn't brave his bad mood just to tell him that.

"Well, uh, you know that new stallion you've been working on breaking?"

Sam froze and his heart dropped to the floor as he stared in complete shock for the space of two seconds. "She wouldn't!" he blurted, but he knew better and was already rising to his feet and barreling out the door. He knocked Ben sideways and didn't even notice in his haste to get to the small paddock where the stallion had been isolated.

The magnificent horse, simply called Devil, would eventually be an asset to the ranch, but he was untrained yet and had an evil temper the likes of which Sam had never seen before. There had been a few injuries and after that he didn't want anyone else taking the risk. Until he had the time to put in, the horse was being kept separate and everyone had been warned to keep away.

He'd even made a special point to be firm with Charlie because he'd seen her eagerness the second she'd laid eyes on the stallion. Most of the men had seen the trouble that horse could be and didn't need much warning to stay away, but not Charlie, of course.

Except Charlie didn't like to do what she was told. "Why the hell didn't anyone stop her!" he barked as he got to the corral and found half of his crew standing around watching the stallion stomping the ground in warning while the girl tried to get closer to him.

"We tried!"

"Told her no one was allowed in there except you, boss. She wouldn't listen!"

"We couldn't exactly stop her, Sam. I mean she kinda owns the place now."

There was a chorus of other protests all of which painted a pretty clear picture of what had happened. Charlie had been told no, and Charlie didn't like to be told no, so she'd used him snapping at her as an excuse to go ahead and do what she wanted anyway. As the Rancher's daughter the men assumed she was now in charge, and no one wanted to be too forceful about stopping her.

It hadn't occurred to him that it would be necessary to make the real situation transparent and he hadn't wanted to embarrass her by making a general announcement that

Charlie had no authority. Obviously, he'd have to fix that misinformation later, but first he needed to get her out of there before she got herself killed. "Charlotte McGee, you get your ass away from that horse right now!" he shouted.

He saw the scared look on her face as she turned but she quickly switched it to an expression that had 'make me' all over it. She knew how to play the haughty boss's daughter card all too well and it used to work, but things had changed.

"You've got three seconds to get out of there or I'm coming in after you, and you won't like what happens if I have to do that, Charlie." His voice was dangerously angry, but the volume was carefully controlled. He felt like shouting but didn't want to startle the stallion and going inside to get her would run the same risk, so he was hoping to scare her out on her own.

"Don't be ridiculous, Sammy. You know how good I am with horses, besides I've just as much right here as you do," she said with a sniff. She continued her slow progress across the ground, one hand flat out in front of her holding an apple she was using to tempt Devil closer.

The horse's nostrils flared, and he looked interested in the treat. He took a slow step towards her and she smiled with confidence. "See?"

"Charlie," the name was forced out through gritted teeth. "That horse isn't just *called* Devil; he *is* a devil. He bites and kicks anyone who gets close to him. Now, I want you to back up, slowly." He was managing to keep his voice down to avoid upsetting the high-strung stallion, but Devil didn't deal well with sudden movements either and there were so many ways this could go dangerously wrong.

His heart was pounding so hard he thought everyone around him could probably hear it. He was terrified he was about to watch the love of his life get trampled, and her response was to laugh.

Her peal of amusement rang out and it startled Devil. He tossed his head, snorting nervously at the unaccustomed sound. Anyone else would have seen how temperamental the stallion was, but Charlie was too convinced she was right. Raised on a ranch and around horses her whole life she *should* have known better, but she wasn't paying attention to her instincts.

Sam could see it was going to go badly. From the hushed voices around him he knew he wasn't the only one. "Get over to the other side and see if you can distract him. Use apples, he likes those." He didn't look around to see who was obeying him, but he heard them move as he carefully lifted the gate latch and let himself inside. He left it ajar as he moved in, closing in on the pair one step at a time.

Devil had to split his concentration between the girl and her tempting snack, and the men who were making a big fuss at the far end with even more interesting treats. Sam was the least interesting target which was exactly how he wanted it. He stepped up behind Charlie and was just about close enough to grab her when she noticed him.

He reached out and she jerked away, in the direction of the horse, of course, with a loud "Hey!" The sudden movement was too much for the animal and he reared up on his hind legs with a loud whinny of irritation. His front hooves came down hard right where Charlie was standing—but Charlie wasn't there anymore.

Sam had snatched her off her feet and tossed her over his shoulder in one swift movement before taking off at full speed towards the open gate. The sound of angry hoofbeats thundered behind them as the horse chased after. A quick-thinking ranch hand slammed the gate shut the second they were through, and the stallion skidded to a halt, snorting loudly with frustration.

Scheme foiled, Devil wandered back to the center of the

corral and began nosing at the abandoned apple while pretending to be the most innocent thing on four legs. There was a certain smugness to the innocence. He loved making people run from him; it was his favorite trick. He'd broken a man's leg already with that little *game*.

Sam dropped his struggling burden on her feet, out of breath and nearly in a panic over how close he'd come to watching her get trampled. He didn't expect a thank you from her, but the last thing he expected was for her to start telling him off at full volume in front of the whole crew.

His eyes widened in shock, and then began to narrow with every word that came out of her mouth. By the time she'd managed a complete sentence, his eyebrows were practically meeting in the center of his forehead. His lips were pressed closed in a firm line to hold back what he wanted to say to her.

She paused, waiting for him to say something, and when he just glared at her she started ramping up for another go at him, but he'd had enough.

His head snapped around, flashing an angry look at the watching crowd. "Don't you all got work to be doing? Move your asses!" The order snapped out at a full bellow that sent everyone running for cover, and had the stallion racing off to the other side of the paddock, too. In seconds there wasn't a soul in sight except the two of them.

Startled by the shouting, she stepped back with a wide-eyed look of surprise on her face. Maybe she thought he'd be yelling at her next, or maybe she had another reason for trying to get her defense in before he could open his mouth. "I had every right to be in there! You had no business picking me up and carrying me out like I was some child. Stomping in like that you're lucky you didn't scare the horse into…"

"Shut. Up." He said it coldly, biting off each word, and her expression as her mouth dropped open was satisfying.

He watched her jaw working as she tried to form words, but he wasn't going to let her get that far. "You almost got yourself killed, Charlie. If I hadn't carried you out of there that horse would have stomped you into the ground! Do you know how many men he's bitten or kicked? Four! And that's with them being careful and staying out of his reach. Not one of them was dumb enough to stroll right up to him with an apple in hand!"

"But I…"

"But nothing! Didn't I tell you he was off limits?"

"Yes, but…"

"Did they tell you not to go in there?"

"Well, yeah but…"

"Then you have no excuse, girl. And then, after I save your ass, you're going to tell me off in front of my men? I don't fucking think so!" The words practically vibrated with suppressed fury and it must have been obvious because she started looking more than a little nervous.

She fidgeted, shoving her hands into the deep front pockets of her jeans and hunching her shoulders like a teenager caught sneaking in after curfew. There was guilt underneath it all, but she was still trying to act like she'd been in the right.

"This is still my ranch too!" she said.

Well, he'd expected that to come up. It was probably best to get it out of the way now. "You know what, Charlie? This has absolutely zero to do with whose ranch it is—but apparently you missed the part where your dad put *me* in charge. I wanted us to be able to work together despite that, but I *thought* my partner would be an adult not a spoiled reckless child."

She gasped, "I'm not acting like a child! Who do you think you are?"

He snorted, not bothering to hide his amusement at the

one word she took exception to. "But you *are* spoiled and reckless right?"

"What? No! That's not what I…"

"I don't care what you meant. You and me, Charlie, we're going to come to an understanding right now. Or you know what I'm going to do?" He folded his arms across his chest and glared down at her, waiting for her to ask.

"You think I'm afraid of you? Fine, what will you do then, spank me? Whatever, go ahead then if it will make you feel like a big man." There was a breathless little catch in her voice and damn if he didn't think that's what she was hoping for. Well, she'd asked him to punish her when she needed it; it was obviously past time to take her up on that.

"If I were you, I wouldn't even suggest that right now. I'm *this* close to wearing your ass out with my belt for this stunt, Charlie. In fact, let's make that a definite plan. You're finally going to get the real punishment you've been after. The question is whether I'm going to leave afterwards."

Her eyes flew open wide and he decided to let her chew on that for a while. He forced himself to turn and walk away, knowing if he stayed, he'd do something he'd regret. As much as he wanted to bend her over the nearest convenient object and pull off his belt, he was well aware that people were probably sneaking looks at them while pretending to work, and he had no intention of giving them a show.

Besides he was too pissed to put his hands on her. That would wait until he calmed down and everyone had left for the day. Once they were the only two people on the ranch, he'd take care of business.

Daddy Krampus
Book One of the Krampus Collective

"So, I should call you Krampus? Or is that just a title?" she asked. He stopped and turned back towards her with a frown. For a second, she thought she'd made him angry.

"I don't have a name separate from Krampus. I've never needed one," he admitted. His expression turned thoughtful, and then he smiled. "You can call me Daddy. It seems fitting since I intend to teach you better behavior."

Her mouth dropped open and she stared. "Daddy? But that's . . ." She let the words trail off as her cheeks heated. She knew why some women called dominant men Daddy. It was because they were caretakers, or because they were punishers and her host seemed like he was probably both.

He paused, the smile grew and then he nodded. "Yes, it's suitable. In fact, it's given me the perfect idea of how to handle your punishments."

"I'm not sure I like calling you that. Maybe I could just call you Krampus," she suggested. Daddy seemed too personal, though she wasn't sure why she would feel that way, since she'd never gotten to call her own father that. At least, not that she could recall.

His expression turned cold and for a second, she could have sworn she saw a red glow in his eyes. "You will call me Daddy, and nothing else, Valerie. Don't make it necessary to show you what happens when you disobey me. Do you understand?"

It wasn't a question it was a demand and she gulped. "Y-yes, Daddy."

"Good, I think I need to make something clear to you. Come." He turned and strode off, forcing her to run along behind him. When he stopped, it was by a familiar door. She recognized it because when she'd left the bedroom earlier, she'd noticed the door was painted in the exact shade of purple that was her favorite. It stood out as strange in a castle where everything else was ornate dark wood.

He opened the door and motioned for her to look inside. She gave him a confused look, but did as he said, confirming it was the same bedroom. "I don't understand," she said, as she looked back at him.

"This is the room I created for you to live in this year. This is where girls who are learning to be good, get to stay. Now, you'll see the alternative." He took her by the arm and pulled her down the hall.

Not far from her room was another door. This one was definitely not painted in a lovely deep lilac color. It was a black so dark it seemed to suck her in, and she didn't want him to open it. She didn't want to see what was inside, but she wasn't given a choice.

He took a heavy metal key from his pocket and plunged it into the ornate lock. The door creaked open slowly and although she pressed back against him and dug in her heels, he planted a hand in the center of her back and pushed her over the threshold. What happened next was like something out of a horror movie.

The door vanished behind her and suddenly she was trapped in some kind of dungeon hellscape. There was a distant soundtrack that included screams of pain, and the howls of some large beasts that she knew immediately would enjoy eating her all up. The walls were harsh, rough stone and the only light came from the torches that hung in brackets from the wall. They were spread out too far to light the room decently, and the flickering flames created large swathes of moving shadow that terrified her.

She searched desperately for the way out but couldn't

even find a crack where the door had been. She heard heavy footsteps coming down the corridor towards her and her racing heart stuttered in her chest as she began to panic. Whatever was coming, she didn't want to see.

She banged on the wall with both fists. "Please, I'll be a good girl, Daddy!" She sounded desperate and scared, but she didn't care. She needed to get out before something terrible happened.

And just like that the wall opened and she fell into his arms. She clung to him, her body shaking. "I want the good room. I want the good room," she said, repeating it several more times as he rubbed her back gently.

"I just wanted you to see how different things could be, Valerie. I've made a lot of changes here, especially for you. My normal yearly guest is not treated so well, although to be fair, they generally have a lot more to atone for," he admitted. "But as long as you are a good girl and learn your lessons, you'll never have to worry about what's behind this door."

She nodded quickly. Her grip on him hadn't relaxed, even though her heart rate was slowly dropping. She wasn't entirely sure why she'd been so terrified. She hadn't *seen* anything especially horrible, but there'd been a sense that terrible things did happen there. Things she knew she didn't want to experience.

✳ ✳ ✳

Krampus Sir

Book Two of the Krampus Collective

He's the embodiment of punishment looking for a mate. She's a shallow brat with dreams of influencer fame. Can they learn to love each other in just one year?

When Krampus chooses her from among all the naughty people in the world, he has more than the usual year of punishment in mind. This time he's looking for a mate. A woman who will thrive under his harsh discipline and learn to love him because of it.

When Nia's lies and self-centered behavior hurt the people around her, she ends up on his naughty list. Now she'll learn what it's like to have her dignity stripped away one painful punishment at a time.

But at the end of the year she'll have a choice to make. Return to her life a better person … or remain with the immortal Dominant permanently as his mate.

* * *

Architect of His Desire

He was a Dominant force of nature.

She was desperately looking to turn her life around.

A steamy stand-alone workplace romance, with a spicy power-exchange twist.

This novella is the perfect short read to get your kink and romance fix in. It begins with an extra steamy workplace scene that will reel you in.

* * *

Gifted Affinities

When April took the job, she had no idea what she was getting herself into. One month in a haunted house...how bad could it be? Then she met John.

He's the Dominant lover of her dreams, coaxing her to submit to him by stirring desires she never realized she had. There are just a few problems:

He's *dead.*

She's a *Medium.*

And their **entire** love affair is being recorded by the paranormal investigators that hired her.

A two-book paranormal romance with lots of steamy scenes, D/s, and spanking.

✳ ✳ ✳

A Timeless Love

When Katherine is callously abandoned by her dominant lover, she is heartbroken. She takes the anniversary trip they'd planned to go on together, but it's nothing but misery. As she slowly spirals into self-destructive behaviors she runs into Jack, a handsome stranger with dominant vibes that catch her attention.

When he steps in to save her from her own behavior, it opens up a whole new world of possibility.

This paranormal romance is a complete trilogy with a HEA in the final book. It has power-exchange, graphic sex, and lots of BDSM—mostly of the Domestic Discipline and spanking variety.

EXCERPTS FROM SADIE MARKS

Check out my Sadec series under Sadie Marks. These books feature a race of alien sadists who find their mirror in certain humans of Earth. The warriors are drawn to those humans who can accept pain and turn it into pleasure. It's like a drug to them and they must have more, at any cost.

Surrendering to Her General

"You understand what's about to happen?" the examiner said. Mrs. Harshaw, according to her laminated badge, was an older professional-looking woman with greying hair tucked up in a neat bun at the back of her neck. She looked like a sweet grandmother type and it seemed at odds with the things she'd just been explaining.

"Y-you're going to do things to me to see how I react," Kenzi said, hesitating over the exact words because she found them impossible to say. She hoped her vague response would be enough for the other woman; it wasn't.

Mrs. Harshaw shook her head firmly. "Please be specific, Kenzi. We need to be sure you know exactly what's going to happen here. We don't want any unpleasant surprises on either side," she said. Her stern look softened the tiniest bit after a second, and she added, "I know this is difficult to talk about, but, well, let's be honest, if you can't even answer the questions—experiencing it is going to be impossible, right?"

Kenzi sighed, nodding her reluctant agreement. There was that, but when she'd fantasized about these things, it had been in such a different environment. All the books she'd read, fiction mostly, had been filled with romance and sexy encounters—not clinics where everything would be recorded and studied.

After a second, she forced herself to answer, trying to ignore her flaming face. "All the pamphlet said was testing may include spanking, light bondage, and sexual touching. Y-you explained in more detail, about, um, implements, and y-you said that since I've n-never done these things before, it would start slowly." She looked at Mrs. Harshaw for approval.

"Correct." The older woman hesitated then closed Kenzi's file and pushed it aside as she leaned in. "Listen, I'm not really supposed to tell you every little thing that's going to happen because my superiors feel that listing it out will make it seem too clinical and you won't be able to respond naturally, but I can tell you that the Sadecs enjoy breaking in newbies. People like you, who have the fantasies and desires but have never actually experienced these things, are at the top of their list. It's very rare to find someone who has never been spanked at all, not even during sex, by a lover, or as a child, for punishment. You will be extremely desirable to them."

She paused there, her eyes flicking nervously to the mirror that covered most of one wall. Kenzi had noted it when she'd entered, and because she'd seen a lot of old movies, she had immediately guessed, correctly, that it was a one-way mirror with people or recording devices behind it. Every room she'd been taken to on all her visits had the same type of mirror. Since there were plenty of other, less obvious, ways to watch someone, she had to think it was deliberate. They wanted to remind her that she was being watched.

It had made answering these questions harder, wondering who was back there listening. Mrs. Harshaw seemed to be debating whether or not she'd get in trouble if she said anything else, but after a few seconds, she continued with one last bit of information.

"Your response testing will be extremely brief if your body reacts as strongly as I expect it will. They won't want to 'pop your cherry', so to speak, in a setting like this. They'll want to turn you over to them still inexperienced, because you'll be more valuable," the examiner said. And that was important. Her value mattered to everyone involved because the more she was worth, the more she'd help her planet reach the next tier of rewards.

"So, if you want to avoid the extra embarrassment, just try to relax and let yourself go," the woman advised, keeping her voice low. She sat back immediately and busied herself with the file again as if they'd just been exchanging pleasantries.

Since Kenzi was sitting there in embarrassingly damp panties just from discussing these things, she was pretty sure her body was going to react strongly, too, but the advice was worth remembering. It made sense when she thought about it. Being stressed and tense would mean dragging things out, so they could get what they needed. The quicker she gave in, the faster things would go. She had to admit this wasn't how she pictured her first spanking, though, and no matter how much they tried, it was going to feel clinical.

How could it not when a stranger was about to bend her over and touch her in intimate ways, probably while making notes on a clipboard about her arousal response time. She'd thought the earlier tests had been bad enough, but those had been solo activities at least. Short clips of BDSM videos had played while she sat alone in a small booth, hooked up to monitors that tracked her reactions, and judged which things turned her on. She'd been soaked by the time they'd come to unhook her, but at least she could pretend they didn't know.

What she had pictured wasn't exactly what she found when she was led to a room for the final test. The rest of the facility resembled the offspring of a hospital and an office building, but this room was straight out of a BDSM novel. She stopped short in the doorway with a little gasp, staring at the furniture, covered in black leather, and the display of implements that covered an entire side of the room. The only things that seemed off were the pristine white walls, which matched the rest of the building.

The examiner chuckled. "I know, shocking, isn't it? It seems to help set the mood with many people, though. Go on inside," she said, giving Kenzi a little nudge.

Kenzi obediently stepped into the room, turning as she moved to see everything. When she was facing the door, she gave the other woman a curious look. "Are you the one who…" she trailed off, looking uncertain.

"Am I the one who's going to test you? No, dear, not me. I just do the interviews; they've hired professionals for this part. It's very important that there aren't any mistakes about these things; after all, five years is a long time to regret your choice, and if you can't enjoy pain, then you will definitely not enjoy being a slave for them," Mrs. Harshaw pointed out gently.

"But…I thought they'd take volunteers anyway, even if they didn't get turned on?" Kenzi asked.

The woman hesitated and then nodded. "In some cases, yes. Some Pain Receivers don't experience arousal from the pain, but they still need it. We rarely pass those types when they are inexperienced like you are, though, dear. In most situations, those are people who have lived a lifestyle where they've received pain frequently and found it necessary," she explained.

"Oh. I guess that makes sense," Kenzi replied. She tucked her hands into her pockets to still the shaking as her eyes were drawn to the wall of implements—whips and paddles mixed with more mundane items like hairbrushes and wooden kitchen spoons. Almost every possible item that could be used to spank someone hung there and a shiver rolled down her spine when she pictured feeling them.

She knew many people had specific items that they hated or loved so it made sense there'd be so many to choose from. There had been questions on her forms about that, but she'd had to leave them blank because she'd never actually felt any of them. All she could answer was which ones had been a focal point in her fantasies, and that was a pretty wide selection. She wondered what they'd pick to use on her now.

"Just go ahead and get undressed, Kenzi. You can keep your panties on if having them removed is part of your fantasies, but in the end, everything will come off," she said gently. "I just need to know what your preference is for the testing. Male or female?" she asked.

"Oh! I get to choose?" Kenzi asked, surprised that she had the choice. For a second, she wondered if she shouldn't ask for another woman; maybe that would be less embarrassing. She'd always chosen female gynecologists for that reason, but no. This was about getting the best reactions from her body. Her fantasies had always run to alpha males, so it would probably be better to stick with a man. "Male, please."

"Very well; he should be in to take care of you in just a few minutes. Remember, this is about setting the mood and preparing you—don't forget, with the Sadecs, you will be a slave, so you'll want to be obedient when he enters, or he might make it harsher as a lesson," the woman warned her.

Kenzi frowned; she didn't entirely understand what that meant. This was just another test. Granted, it was an odd one that would test her erotic responses, but it was still part of the process. "Am I supposed to pretend I'm a slave for the testing then?" she asked.

The woman gave her an indecipherable look and shook her head. "Kenzi, if your body reacts to this, you won't be pretending. This is the last step. All the paperwork is signed, and you were given the opportunity to change your mind last week. When you showed up this morning, you entered into a binding contract. If what happens here arouses you, you will pass the test, and if you pass, you will belong to them. Good luck, dear," she said. There was a look of compassion on her face as she left the room, closing the door firmly behind her.

Taken by the Renegade (A stand-alone companion)

She could feel them watching her. Not really a surprise, since she was currently spread-eagled and mostly naked, with her bare breasts pressed against a giant x-shaped St. Andrew's cross that was positioned on a small dais in the main room of the club. People tended to stop and watch the show when anyone was on the cross, and the stage was positioned as a focal point so everyone could see.

Being the center of attention at the club didn't bother her anymore. She was used to it, but it did make her hyper-aware of every reaction, and deep down, there was a certain smugness in knowing that she was able to control how she responded to each stroke. There was more than a little pride there, and sometimes it pushed her to go further than she actually enjoyed when she knew she had an audience.

She didn't always want to play hard and rough; on some nights, she was happy with just enough heat and sting to make her float. A belt across her ass, a good paddling, or even being restrained in an uncomfortable position with tight ropes could fill her needs. But tonight, she was in the mood for the kind of heavy play that the cross was built for, so it had only been a matter of finding a partner who had the skills. It hadn't taken her long to spot the new face in the crowd.

He was tall, a head taller than everyone around him, and handsome in an understated way. He was definitely not a sub or bottom—not with that aura of dominance he radiated. The arms he crossed over his chest had enough muscle to show where the shirt tightened around his biceps. His eyes skimmed lightly across the room, searching for something or someone. She decided that must be her and made a point of catching his attention.

The conversation had been short, just long enough to exchange the important details. He had a bag full of gear, and when she asked what he was carrying, he'd gestured for her to look for herself. It took exactly ten seconds to find the single-tail whip right on top, and after that, she lost interest in seeing what else he had. She held it out to him. "You any good with this?" she asked, and when the answer was a cruel grin spreading across his lips, she turned and started toward the unused cross, determined to claim the spot before anyone else did.

If it bothered him that she led the way, he didn't comment on it. If he had, she would have looked elsewhere for her fun. She stripped off her shirt and jeans next to it without hesitation, knowing no one would blink twice in a BDSM club where half the players were in some stage of undress.

She pressed against the cross with her back to him and waited as he tightened the cuffs around her wrists and ankles with the ease of someone who'd done it before. She wasn't risking much playing with a stranger, not in the club, but she was glad to see him checking to make sure they were loose enough for circulation but tight enough to hold her. It meant he had experience to go with the pretty toys.

He brushed her hair forward over her shoulder to leave her back completely bare and leaned in. "How much can you handle?"

"Tonight? A lot. Don't go easy on me; I'm in the mood for something merciless," she said. She turned her head so he could see that she meant what she said. He managed an expression that was both delighted and ravenous at the same time, and with a laugh, he moved away.

The wood felt cool against the bare skin of her torso, and as she shivered, the cuffs restraining her arms over her head jangled softly. The first lash of leather came down, leaving a fiery stripe diagonally across her back, and she had cause to test their strength. The sudden biting sting made her jerk in surprise, and she probably would have stumbled backward and maybe fallen to the dirty floor if the cuffs hadn't held her in place, but they did their job and she was the perfect target for the next stroke to land a second later.

He wasn't using a light hand. There was no slow build; the new Dominant had taken her at her word when she'd told him she could take a lot. For just a second, she considered saying 'yellow' to slow him down a little—if only because the first two were already harder than the ending strokes for most of the newcomers to the club.

But Sam had a reputation for never using her safeword, and she wasn't about to blow it now just because someone had listened to her for once. The regulars knew, of course, that when she said she wanted merciless, she wasn't looking to be teased with light flicks that barely stung, but even most of them weren't willing to give her what she really wanted right out of the starting gate.

Oh, they'd work up to it eventually, but when she was in a mood like this, that slow build could be as aggravating as an itch she couldn't reach. She often had to grit her teeth to keep from being too much of a smart-ass at times like that. A little sass might get her smacked harder, but too much and she'd insult a Top; that never went well. Either they'd walk away, or worse, they'd simply refuse to give you what you wanted at all and the slow, almost gentle, strokes would never lead to where she really needed them to go.

She craved pain sometimes, needed it like she needed air, and nothing made her pussy dripping wet faster than a strong dominant with a single-tail whip who knew how to use it. She wasn't going to wuss out and ask him to slow down just because he'd listened to her and went straight for the good stuff. A third and then a fourth blow came down with searing, but controlled, overhand strikes, and her muscles shook with strain.

Damn, it felt like fire raining down on her naked skin and she fought the urge to yelp when the fifth one swung low and wrapped around her hips. The tip of the whip landed on the front of her thigh. She threw her head back, hissing through her teeth as a hard pulse of sexual desire began to throb low in her body. Her skin tightened and she could feel goose-bumps rising everywhere.

She was so focused on her body that the sound of the whip cracking seemed distant, almost unconnected to the sensations rolling through her body. She was thoroughly grounded in the physical at the moment. The sultry air, just a little bit too warm from all the bodies filling the club, caught her attention as it brushed across her highly sensitive flesh and a shudder rolled down her spine.

The leather landed, crossing to wrap around from the other side, and the searing line dragged her attention there. Her back arched and then itched as sweat beaded and rolled down over the welts. It felt so good, so right, as it forced the real world away. Her hopes, her broken dreams, her memories of a childhood gone wrong—all of it had been weighing too heavily on her lately. That was what brought on these moods and was the reason she needed something harsher, crueler than usual, because none of it mattered when she was under the lash.